'The Tyranny of Talin'

The land of Waller Trilogy

Book One

Best wishes
from
Richard Todd

Author: R W Todd

The Tyranny of Talin

By R W Todd

<u>The War of Twilight</u>
The Madness of Avlon Klynn
For it's a Hard Line

***Within A Single Moment**

<u>The Land of Waller</u> Trilogy
The Tyrany of Talin
***Dead Men Don't Die**

One of the things I enjoy the most is writing, I just want to say a thank you for every one that has not only helped me make this possible. But to those who live on in my heart, and to those that are within my family.

You have my thanks.
Richard

One

Flight of Fear

The sun shone on a nice clear day as flowers reached for the sky, though there was a slight breaze from the north. It cooled the air somewhat, but still it felt like home. The last time the young lad had remembered , but something had caught his attention which was on his right. He glanced over to see what it was as he noticed several large beings rushing over to him , Flinlie stood stock still as the creatures kept on running toward him. Pure blank fear filled his soul as he realized of what the creatures were after. He hadn't a clue of how to escape, he looked around trying to figure out how to get away from them. They surrounded him on all sides, a massive army of trolls and Orcs marched toward him. Some were running while others were just walking, but their goal lay before them.

Suddenly he felt smoehting grab onto him, he looked to his shoulder to see claws on both sides of him. Neither of them pinching him but at least they were holding him in place. He paniced as he began to yell and waved his arms frankedly trying to get free from whoever had him.

"Help me" he cried as he now noticed that he was being lifted up into the sky."Some one help" he now yelled as tears ran down his face once panic stricken in him once again only to hear a voice above him. It sounded as if it were friendly, but yet he puzzled over of what it might be.

"What do you think I'm doing" the bird informed him. As it flew over the beasts, Flinle looked up to see a gaint bird.

"Put me down" Flinlie demanded not pleased by being up so high in the sky. He moved his feet and he could tell that he wasn't going to be set down anytime soon. He brefly looked down, then closed his eyes wishing he wasn't there. Flinlie hated hights, he could feel something in his stomach and it unsettled him.

"Not yet" the roc said as it flew on.

"Why not?"Flinlie retorted.

"Those Orc's want you",the roc replied as the bird spotted a forest several miles away.

"Doesn't explain this" the nineteen year old

exclaimed feeling light headed from the high attitude.

"Sorry, I guess I should explane. That horde is following us as we speak. So until night falls we can't land".

Flinlie looked down again and saw the horde. Bile filled his mouth, and the sight still unnerved him. He swallowed down his panic. He wanted to scream but found that his lungs felt as though they were on fire.

"Question" Finlie said, biting down on his fear of hights as he was trying not to vomit since he was getting air sick.

"What is it?"the bird wondered.

"I just looked do…" he stopped speak as he moved his hand near his mouth, "plaa" the bird heard the boy throw up at last.

"Air sick, you'll be fine soon" the bird stated with

concern then decided to circle the horde which made it even worse.

"Fine we'll land in Hardwood forest, they won't be able to follow us in" as the bird circled twice as the teenager barfed, which hit five Orc's in the head a moment later.

"I'm Corp" the bird annouced "What's yours?".

"Friends call me Flinlie but ny real name is Gemmel" as the boy wiped his mouth with his hand. Landing moments later Gemmel looked at the bird for the first time.

"Wow, I didn't know you were a hawk"

"I'm not a hawk" the bird told him "We orginate from them yes, but not a hawk" the boy studied him for a moment.

"If not a hawk, then what are you?"

"Roc" the bird said as he saw the boy laugh.

"What"s so funny?kid" Corp asked.

Once the boy stoped laughing he just looked at the Roc for a second.

"A rock is on the ground with grass surrounding it, you sir- I mean bird are no rock" Gemmel anounced. The great bird smiled which frightened the boy since the beak was open and with narrow eyes.

"Your right I'm not a rock but I'm a roc" Corp said which the teen looked puzzled. "Let me explane, you discibed a hard stone of grey known as a rock. I sir, am a Roc. A giant bird, known to many. It's spelled without a k".

Gemmel took in the information, but now noticed elves within the tree's which looked at them.

"People" Gemmel indecated as the Roc swung his head to the left seeing his friemds.

"Their friends of mine, they don' like humans much, but your important to us" the bird told the boy as he spread his wings. "I will be back" Corp said as he flew off a moment later.

The Elves didn't appear at all, but when it was high noon a small child came out into the clearing with some food. Placing it down a moment later, Gemmel smiled at the young girl.

"You shouldn't be afriad young one" he assured her that stood in front of him. She stiffened in fright and saw his hand stick out.

"Don't you know about hand shakes" Gemmel said as he watched the girl's eyes moved slightly and her mouth opened.

"N- no" she answered weakly. He smiled at her and placed his hand at his side.

"It's a sign of friendship, to show that I'm

unarmed of any weapon".

She blinked and looked at the fruit that she had given him. "I see why your kind protects this forest, it's because they embrace nature" Gemmel said then smiled to himself. "I adore nature as do several of mime own do. Not all, some want it dead and gone, so don't fear me" he said with a pleasing voice as he placed an apple slice on his tongue, noticing a grown Elf standing beside the girl for the first time.

"I'm Kathorine" she said then looked up at the male elf. "Father" she said and he nodded. She turned to go only to turn back a bit, she winked at him.

"Nice to meet you Gemmel" the male Elf said as Gemmel straighened at the mention of his name, puzzled at what had just happened. Seeing her leave the male elf sat down in front of him.

"We have been expecting you for sometime,sir." As he extended his hand "Bracer" he introduced himself. "Corp has been looking for you for two years now" seeing the puzzlement in the humans eyes. "All will be explaned in due time".

*   *   *

Fighting his way through the crowd toward his companions the young man had to push his way through.

"Watch it" someone yelled but Tucker hadn't noticed the woman in front. Pushing her to the side, he didn't noticed where his hands were. She reached out with her hands and a crackling sound could be heard.

"That hurt" he mumbled and the noise dropped silent.

"You should never touch a woman's breast" she said as he blushed at the thought.

"I-er" he replied a bit ashamed at what he did.

"What?" she yelled at him.

"Sorry, so sorry maim" he replied guilty at what he had done. But she noticed a man behind the boy.

"Reid" she said with a smile on her face."been along time, darling" as she battered her eye lashes at him.

" I see you've met Tucker" Reid said as she smiled at him.

"Of caurse, I should have realized he was your son" she declaired but Reid only smiled seeing the humor in the statement as he shook his head.

"He's not my son, Tucker here is my scout" Reid informed her then leaned in to whisper in her ear.

"He's older than the two of us put together". He pulled back from her.

"He's Immortal" she said with surprise.

"Rachel, not so loud" Reid said as he glanced around the room hoping no one heard. "Join me at the table" he said as he walked over to it with Rachel following behind him.

"Rachel" a dark haird man beamed as he stood up.

"Hi, Bobby" Rachel said then kissed him lightly on the cheek, tucker noticed the barniad with the drinks.

"Here we go" the dirty haird blond said as hse set down the drinks.

"So what are we drinking too?" Rachel asked with wonderment.

"We saved a village a fort night ago" Tucker

piped up. “There were Orc’s everywhere, which were killing man and their families. I reckon their looking for something or someone”. Reid shook his head “we were able to rescue half the village” Tucker finished. Rachel lifted her glass which held red wine.

“To victory” she said cheering them on. Several minutes later Reid gout up from his chair.

“I’ll be back, the Guild would be expecting our find” he said then dashed off, out through the door.

“Guild” Rachel said puzzled by the news “which guild is this and what’s he have to give them?”. Bob smiled and glanced at his two friends who nodded.

“Someone stole a jewel from the thieves Guild a few weeks ago and they hired us to retreave it for them” Bob said as he took a sip from his mug.

The Tyranny of Talin

"Here we go" as Reid passed over the jewel to the leader of the thieves guild.

"Thanks Reid, I'm in your debt" the leader said then remembered the information. "A man call Jhet wants to hire you, look for him in Dale's Tavern".

" Thanks Red, I'll be back when I'm done with him" then turned to go.

"Hold on, Reid" the bald headed man said. Reid turned back "be very careful with Jhet, do or say the wrong thing will cost you your life" Reid turned pale at the news.

"Thanks for the warning" he muttered and left the area, unsure if he should be helping an assassin. Reid and his band of misfits normally stayed in the shadow of the law, but helping an assassins was a different kind of mess.

His contacts ini this village of Floren were old friends

of his, dealing with strangers was something else all togther which meant trouble.

Toothby his younger brother crossed the line three years ago which Reid would never forget the scum that had killed him. To this day Reid had been looking for his brothers killer.

Walking back into the tavern he noticed his friends having a good time.

"I'm Jhet" a male said not smiling which startled the man.

"I, oh. Yes I was told about you" Reid stated then shifted his eyes to an empty table so not to be heard. Jhet followed the traveler hoping no one would be the wiser."I hear you want me to do an assignment" .

"Yes, Indeed" the assassin said. Reid could not

tell if the man had hair but his nose stood out, big as a pig so to speak. He wore black armer over tights. "I'm not in the habit of hiring Rogues or headhunters, so be patient. I have been contacted by a warlock that has lost his son".

"I don't do humans" Reid told the man.

"This kid's special"

"How special?"

" Don't ask questions, that could kill you or your friends" Jhet warned him.

"I don't like assassins" Reid hissed angrily.

"How's four thousand sound" Jhet said trying to ignor Reids outburst. He eyed the assassin, it was a whole a lot of money for him or it might involve trouble for him. He liked to live dangerously.

"We'll do it" he annouced "what's this kids name?" Reid dared to ask. The assassin leaned in to whisper.

"His friends call him Flinlie, that's all you need to know" then disappeared into the crowd. Stepping up to his table his friends looked up at him.

"Having a disagreement" Reid said seeing the tension .

"Just a small one" Rachel said "Bob and Tucker are wondering who's the stronger of the two". Reid smiled at the thought.

"Neither" he told them "I'm the stronger, Tucker the wiser, but Bob is the skinner". Rachel laughed at the joke. "Any how we've got a new mission" he told his crew and smiled at the idea. He did'nt want to tell them that an assassin had hired them.

Shifting his eyes slightly, Bobby got up from the table.

The Tyranny of Talin

"Bout time too, I just spent all of our money" Bobby told them. The others glared at him not happy at all, Reid grabed him by the collar.

"You did what?" Reid thundered with anger. Bobby swallowed at the anger that Reid had. "I- I lost it, buying all the drinks" Bobby claimed. Reid pushed him away, Bob tumbled and slabed into a nearby table. Every drink spilled, the six men that sat there stood up. Bob could see they were big strong men with the same hair do.

" You'll pay for our drinks" one of the men said.

"I got no money" Bob sputtered out. Which didn't go over to well. All six men strienched their necks and pounded their fist into an open palm.

"Hold up mates, I don't think beating up a scum bag that has no money left doesn't mean you should kill the man" Reid stated as he walked up to them.

"Besides, how would it look if his friends left him on his own" the other two nodded.

"He, your friend?" a big muscle man asked.

"He night" Reid answered then winked at Tucker and Rachel.

"Then die" the muscle man said but the man stood frozen before he could do anything. As of his friends were frozen as well.

"Thanks Reid" Bob said as he walked over to him.

"We better walk out" Reid told the group then heard the muscle man shout over to them.

" I ain't done with you yet, I will have my vengance" then spat out only to see it frezze in midair which traveled back to his tongue.

Rachel smiled at the sight and gigled inspit of the

man.

"Don't try to fight it, it only gets worse" Rachel said as she glanced at the owner. "Have a good month with them. You can tell them anything you want, just don't give them beer or water". Then left the bar with her companoins.

"Well" the long haird owner said "It looks like you'll be satying with us a while" turning to his wife.

"I see Rachel has improved her magic skills" the dirty blond woman said and leaned over the counter.

"That a witch?" one of the six asked.

Joe shook his head but laughed all the same.

"You messed with a druid, doorbell".

"I'm thirsty" the leader said "pass a beer over dear" she glanced at him.

"It'll kill you , but I will give you something hot".

The frozen man smiled at the thought,

"Your willing to warm me" he said which caught Joe's attention.

"I'll do the warming, handsome" Joe replied as the five laughed at the thought.

"Hot cider it is" Claire said but the leader made a face.

"Cider" he exclaimed not liking the sound to it. "I hate cider"

"It will unfrezze you" Claire answered as she waved her husband over.

"In that case c-cider it is" the leader said then heard his stomack growl "and some food" he added. She looked at him then studied the big fat man, Joe shook his head.

"You could skip a weeks worth of meals" Claire

insulted him but Joe laughed at the man.

"You calling me fat" he howled at her which forced Joe to step up to him with a axe in hand.

"See this axe I'm holding" Joe sad as the man nodded.

"Yes,sir" he growled.

"If you make another comment like that, I'll swear to god I will take your arm off" Joe threatened the man. The six looked around the tavern seeing others whispering and laughing.

"I'm Dale" the leader said defeated by the argument.

* * * *

The wind felt warm to Corp and he knew what to expect from the weather. He could tell just by the smell alone but it also helped out a lot by the wind that helped him fly. Circleing over head he noticed that the Orc's were being slaughtered by the hidden elves. The last Orc fell but something caught Corp's his eye. He circled back the way he had came noticing two Orc,s running away from the scene.

"Begone with you" the mighty Roc roared as he dived at them which stopped the two, they looked at each other at first trying to see who spoke. Neither of them had a clue then they realized something was coming at them with a great speed. They both looked over their shoulders to see a Roc level off, both Orc's were stunned by the huge bird as it changed shape. Human legs appeared then the torso, the head appeared elven in nature, arms appeared as the feathers folded inward.

"I'm Corp what's yours" he asked as he withdrew a glincing sward, he swung it. One Orc fell to the ground as it held its side.

"Your no Roc" one of the two Orc's said. The tip of the sward hit the skin just above the rib cage.

"Tell your master to back off" Corp threatened trying not to have a good time.

"Never we need the boy" an Orc said.

"What the hell for?" the half breed demanded.

"We'll never tell" an Orc said trying to fight off the pain.

"Tell me or I'll press harder" Corp warned the two which glanced at each other which were badly hurt to do anything. The elf pressed even harder trying no t to kill the beast.

"Talin wants his magic to grow sronger, so he can rule all of Waller" one of the Orc's said defeatedly. The half elf looked grim at the mention of the news he puzzled over the clues not sure how it all fit together.

"One more move toward the boy, it'll be open war" he warned the two. The Orc on the ground smiled at the sound of it.

"It'll be a pleasure to kill you half breed" only to feel flesh blood pour out a new wound. The half elf pulled out his sward from the creature then walked away. What the two Orc's didn't know was that the half breed had wounded them badly, but the two walked toward their own camp that was over the next hill.

Glacing over the country, the roc took in the beauty of the land then glanced to his right to see the mounatin regine of Reaya, where the dwarves made their home. Looking down at the forest that he had put Gemmel in. Corp spotted four travelliers in the far distance, he personally knew them.

"Ha, look guys" Bob said as he pointed at the bird in the sky which was coming up to them. Reid noticed the colours of the Roc, he smiled to himself.

"Relax, Bob it's only Corp" he stated then shruged at the thought. He had dealings with the halfbree as far back as he can remember.

Looking almost human a moment later Corp smiled as he finished walking up to them.

"What's up Corp" Reid asked as he shook the mans hand. The half breed looked grim as if something weighed him down.

"Plenty Reid. I need you to do a job for me" Corp said as he folded his arms together.

"Sorry Corp old buddy, we have a mission" Reid replied not willing to take on another job.

"What ever it is. I just don't care, I have one that is more important" Corp stated as Reid only stood there. "Orge's have been ransaking villages lately".

"I heard about that" he replied not careing what it was all about.

"Their after an important human" Corp said which caught Reid's attention. Rachel opened her mouth only to be interupted by Tucker.

"Look half breed, we all ready have a mission..." but Corp shot his hand forward and lifted the immortal off the ground.

"I don't care about your mission, this is more important than what you think" he snapped as he lowered the immortal . Corp explained about the reason, the four looked shocked at the news as Reid ran his fingers through his hair.

"It's not our problem, bird. We're not fighters nor warriors, we collect things or people so we can live" Reid said heatedly then continued. "Get someone else to do your bidding". Corp only smiled at the man unaffected by the mans temper.

"I never did tell you who killed your father didn't I" the bird stated. Reid shook his head

"You never did Corp, but that was the past. What's done is done" Reid said unconvinced by his own words.

"Talin killed your father" Corp finally said, seeing the man go beat red in anger. "Your father was a brave warrior that served your city. He was loyal and had the honor to up hold peace. Then one day he met a man. Talin murdered your father infront of your mother". By this time the bird could see the hatred within the man's eyes. No one spoke for several minutes.

Reid turned his head toward his companions while

his eye lids were slanted in hatered.

"Any of you coming" he wondered but Tucker was a fraid of answering.

"t-t-to do what?" he asked as he backed up a bit hoping not to be hit by his friend.

"To kill Talin" Reid annouced then noticed the weapons in his fiends hands.

"We'll be with you til the end of the earth" Rachel stated as Reid smiled as the others nodded. He turned to see the country side as his blood pumped in exicleration.

"I will avenge my father" Reid said with determination.

Two

By Way of Evil

Glancing over the mountain range, Talin the Terrible let his waist lengh white hair bristle in the wind. He looked back over his shoulder since he heard footsteps behind him. Turning around to focus his attention on the being he smirked.

"So, who sends you?" he said asking the vampire

that now stood before him.

"No one sir. I came to tell you that we have lost a patrol of Orc's" Dodd said as he saw the sun rise, he backed up into the cave to be shielded in the shadows. Away from the harmful sun that could burn him.

"Lost" Talin growled in anger. "To whom and why" he demanded. The vampire swallowed before he answered.

"Corp sir" Dodd replied.

The evil elf stared at him mocking him to the core.

"That Half breed" he hissed with clenched teeth. "I'll make sure he won't be able to do that again" then looked into the vampires eyes. "Kill any that stand in your way. I will get that boy no matter what happens".

Talin got tired of the sight, he walked toward his vampire Lt. Emerging into his private chambers, knives of all sorts lined the walls, he was heavey in armer which he was proud about. A dragon's head was mounted high up on one of the walls, as a small fire was aflame to keep the warmth of the room. He kept on walking, as Dodd followed his master into the main chamber. They stopped, neither of them spoke.

Sounds of footfalls surrounded in the vast chamber where Talin and Dodd stood. Talin glanced at one of the walls seeing nothing but shadows.

"I'm not ready" he said in fury but the shadows took a step further. A single Shadow formed a leg, as it reached out into the air. Breaking from the wall, the shadow was now in fill form. You could see why they were called the Shadows, it was like looking at a dark figure.

"You don't call the shot's Talin. We do, you may command our army but if you try anything foolish we will be forced to kill you" the female shadow warned him. Talin grew tired by the threats that the shadow race had been dishing out lately. He rolled his eyes while staring at his first officer then decided to face his visitors.

Talin had grown to tallerate them, but he was mad out of his mind.

"Go ahead kill me" he dared them "someone or something will replace me no matter what you do". The shadows looked at each other, their faces hidden in shadow so not to be known or Identified.
One of them stepped up to him a second later.

"We will give you one more chance Talin, Screw

up you will join your father" a male shadow threatened, the hatred in his eyes bowled up Talin wanted to lash out at the single shadow. Instead he turned away "leave me" Talin said calmly.

The shadows left the chamber leaving the elf with his follower. Balls of fire shot out from his hands, hitting everything in sight. The vampire that stood there was stunned by the fury and was amazed by the distruction that his master left behind.

"That vampire" Talin finally said "is what I can do". The elf glanced over his shoulder to see that he was alone at last. "I will get control of all the lands" he snarled. "No one will be able to stop me".

* * *

Standing over Gemmel, the elf known as Bracer dicided to sit down.

"Your friend came back while you were sleeping"

the Elf leader stated and the nineteen year old looked excited.

"Is he still here?" Gemmel asked but the Elf replied with a small smile.

"He had to leave, but will be back at the end of the week" Bracer assured him then leaned back on the wall. Sitting up a second later, he slowly got to his feet.

"Well" the young boy said "I can't stay in bed all day" then walked out into the village. The leader followed him out.

"Don't wonder out of the forest" Bracer warned and the boy nodded as he passed the only shop in town then disappeared into the forest a second later. Looking around the forest and the underbush, Gemmel peered over a tree branch that was in his way.

"What" he exclaimed as his eyes settled on the old village that had ancient written all over it. The buildings were in ruins, he tock a step furhter "wow" he said "I wonder what happened here.

"Talin" a voice said coiming from his right, he looked over to see a beautiful female with long red hair. He had seen her once before but he couldn't place it.

"What?" he asked in puzzlement since he didn'y hear the word right.

"This used to be Talins home" the girl snapped.

"How would you know?" Gemmel stated not sure if he should believe a word of it.

"Because it used to be mine as well" her remark came which stung him as her eyes looked hard. "He killed everyone" but she didn't stop there. "His family was the ones that lived through the massicure" she pointed to the hut that lay off to his right. "When I came back from a near by village, I found all the bodies. Every day upon every hour I cried as I buryed all of them".

He studied her and her movements, he was horrified at the thought.

"I'm so sorry" he implied. She walked over to him and asked.

"Why are you here?" she wondered.

"I'm making a map of the forest" Gemmel replied as he held the paper up to her.

"You haven't done much" she said then setting her eyes on him once more.

"The elves asked me to make this map since they are too busy protecting this forest" he replied as she nodded.

"Ah, all ways to busy protecting them sleves than us" she replied in a huff then added "I'm Linda".

" Flinlie- sorry, I'm Gemmel" he replied as he extended his hand as she smiled at him and at the small joke.

"So Flinlie- Gemmel" Linda said trying to see which name he really replied to.

"It's just Gemmel" he assured her "friends call me flinlie for some reason of which I really don't know".

"Well Gemmel which village are you staying" Linda asked in wonderment.

"It's over a mile from here" he said as he pointed towards the center of the forest. "I don't know what it's called, but I guess Corp will tell me one day"

She lifted her head a little, a firm tightening of the lips could be seen.

"He will" Linda assured him as she carefully studied the area hoping that they were both safe.

"I take it you know each other" Gemmel said not sure why Linda was studying the old ruin of a town.

"That we do, he's on a mission for me at the moment. He won't be back for over a week" then added a second later. "I'm sure you will go a little further one day but just stay on the path. It ends at Londer, a village where I stay once in a while". She turned away from him to walk back.

"I sure will" Gemmel called out and rolled the paper map back up. Gemmel felt too excited to do anything else for the day, he passed two streams before he realized that he was lost.

"Well, well lads, look what we have here" an orc said as he came up to the boy. Gemmel now noticed he wasn't in the forest anymore.

"Stay away" Gemmel said as he back up.

"Or you'll what, hurt us" as the four advanced toward the boy who was frightened by the orcs. Powerful hands grasped the boy as the four Orcs looked upon the five travelors.

"Tank" one of the orcs said "kill these traders while I grab the boy" the leader turned around with the boy and urged him to get back into the forest.

Gemmel was half way back to the forest when he spotted an orc running beside. He ran as fast as possible, he noticed that one of the orcs were running on all four it was as though it was a half breed of some sort. He kept on running wishing that he had not had left the forest.

He looked to his left, seeing the orc right beside

him. The orc jumped toward him, Gemmel ducked hoping that the orc would not hit him.

Gemmel ran faster, more than a human could, it was as though he were a superhuman but he wasn't.

"Almost there" he muttered as he noticed the elves up ahead, but he could see Braver in a tree not to far from him.

"You won't escape me boy" an orge snarled as Gemmel jumped into the forest and landed onto his feet. Breathing hard, he rolled out of the way as several arrows wized passed him. But the orges rounded in a half circle then got to his two feet once more.

"This ain't over human" the orge called out as he pulled out an arrow from his thigh, it howled in agony.

The Tyranny of Talin

As flames surrounded the four adventured, it kept off the orcs from advancing. Earlier Rachel had mentioned the plan, so far the ring of fire had kept them off. But Reid could tell that she was getting tired by the second.

"Drop the righ of fire" he commanded but she shot him an angry look.

"No" she shot back but he ignored her, he could tell that they were going to lose.

"We're all most there, we can hold them off". Reid said as he gazed at her, the orcs were mad they tried to get near them. Reid had no idea that the boy he touched was the one that they were looking for.

She liked the idea of resting but Rachel knew she had to hold them off a bit longer. Must keep going, she thought urging herself to keep going.

They weren,t to far from from the forest that

Gemmel was in, she faltered since her magic was drianing. The group could see the end in sight, Reid choped at an orc, Tucker ducked as an orc swung a punch it missed him just by an inch. Bobby threw his small knives at them but the pressing attack was too much for them. With in a few minutes they were drained and beaten the orcs had them as they lumbed closer. A few of them burst into flames as others were turned to dust. Reid noticed the line of dust and at the end of theline a beautiful young woman stood. Her wild red hair, blew in the wind as Reid could sence magic in the air. The rest of the orcs turned to see her.

"May Ig forgive me" she whispered then pushed her hands out, banishing nearly half of them to dust.

"Come forword" the red haird urged them as Reid and the rest of his friends slowly made their way to her, Reid noticed that she wore a greenish top and pants that was way to big for her. Her feet had sandels on. "You must hurry" she told them as several orcs crested a small hill, seeing that the group had survived the onslaught.

Entering the forest a minute later, the elf woman noticed that Rachel was limping. "Your hurt" she exclaimed as she looked at the injury, Reid now saw the two arrows imbeded into her right shoulder. He looked mad but he needed to be calm, he told him self that he had to since it wasn't there fault in the first place. It was his, he wanted to help the young man which got them in this situation in the first place.

"Will she live" Reid wondered as he matted his hair down with his hand since it was a mess. He knelt down on the ground as he looked at Rachel. Reid wanted to cry, he didn't want to lose his friend at all, he was beside himself with greaf.

"She'll live" the elf said assuring him as they locked eyes, both knew each other and yet neither of them said a proper hello. Reid watched as Linda tended to his friend, bringing out the arrows and the arrow heads from Rachels still body.

"How did you do that?" he questioned not sure why there was no sign of pain.

"Do what?" Linda asked as she cleaned the wounds with some water that she powered over the area.

"By taking out the arrows without her screaming" he questioned trying to make sence of it all. Linda smiled weakly, she had to keep her secret from her old and dearest friend.

" S-h-e p-pressure pointed" Rachel said with clenched teeth lying to him about the truth since she was helping the elf out more than anything. Reid watched his old friend walk over to the river to wash her hands, he wen over to her to speak to her without the others hearing.

"I saw you needed help, that's why I came out. Besides Corp told me to expect you" Linda said to Reid who smiled at her with warm eyes.

"That's not why I came over, they don't know about us. I rather keep it a secret for now" Reid said as he glanced over to his friends then back at her once more.

"You haven't told them what you are, nor about us. You should, cause one day they will have a shock" Linda warned as she winked at the human with a playful smile. Reid almost laughed at the thought, both of them were tempting temptation.

Getting back to the group, Reid and Linda walked

side by side with each other. As Tucker watched the two, he smiled to himself since he was immortal. Not only that but he could hear a converation a mile away, he knew Reids secret and wasn't willing to tell it to anyone. He looked at the two who stepped up.

"Corp wants all of you to seek something that maybe very important" Linda began as she looked at the makeshift goup. She could tell that the immortal had heard their conversation but she also kept quiet. it's the broken sword".

The four could not believe their luck since they were given another quest on their shoulders, but Reid smiled weakly knowing that he must get the sword to finish Talin.

"We all ready have a quest?' Rachel demaned, as she got to her feet. "We're trying to find a young man".

"We will finish that later, Rachel. We have more important things to worry about now" Reid was trying to point out but Rachel would not let it go.

"Your telling me that finding a sword is more important than this boy. That you Reid, the so called king of our land has…" Reid flinched, as he stared at her in shock. "that's right I know all about you and Linda, your so called elf lover. Now tell me what's more important than this boy?".

Tucker looked shocked at the out burst but not at the words. Bobby laughed nervously since he was an old friend of Reids, he had never told him that he had figured it out. Reid looked at everyone now, they all knew in one way or another.

"That's right I'm a make shift king but not a full one, I never wanted it in the first place. This sword is more important than you think, it can defect Talin if used right. This boy you speak of, he's nothing to us at the moment". He turned to his girlfriend eyes eyes were lite up with glee, he stood straighter than before. His presence called forth, his commanding ways took over as he studied his next words. "I will find this sword and I promise you that I will defect the evil that plague this land, our country. Men will rise against Talin and many others in my name alone. They will fear me". Reid turned away from the elf that was only a hundred and twenty. Usually Elves would stick together but in this case, it was entirely different.

Everyone was afriad of Talin since he was growning in power, and it wasn't just the good creatures it was also the evil ones as well. The group turned to leave only to be stopped as Linda called out to them.

"Wait, your druid is still hurt, she must rest for the night" Reid nodded in agreement as he looked back to her with a smile. He was pleased that she had insisted for them to stay.

The longing in his eyes spoke volumes as did hers but they knew that they couldn't since he had his friends with him.

* * *

Darkness hang in the castle chamber, its features could not be seen since it was glade in darkness. But only two figures that stood in the middle were were in a deep discossion. Their words were unknown to any since they didn't speak any of the languages except their own since they were part of the Shadow order, a single shadow lumbed over them with out their knowledge. The one man could see the pillers, his master looked up into the stands than back athis own brother.

"Talin is taking too long, he should invade Waller now" he snarled but his brother shook his head.

"He's bent on finding this boy, until he has him then he'll invade" Cole said calmly.

"NOT GOOD ENOUGH" his brother shouted out seeing that his older brother was a wimp after all. "Convince him the boy is unimportant besides Gemmel has no idea where he truly comes from" then paused to think as he lowered his eyes. Suddenly a thought sprang up, red eyes looked straight at the shadow and he smiled evilly. "If he wants him bad enough, then why don't we capture him". His older brother hated the idea.

The Tyranny of Talin

"No, I will be a party to this" Cole claimed not sure where this was going. He sensed something was wrong but he couldn't tell what it was. His younger brother moved off annoyed by Cole's attitude.

"Why do you test my patients? Brother" he looked into Cole's hard cold eyes hoping that there was hope for them.

"Aride, we're in this together as a whole. Talin isn't one of us, he could never measure up to us even if he tried". Cole pointed out as his brother started to move off. Ready to face the battle once more. He turned a moment "Cole, you're a bitter disappointment" Aride said coldly. Leaving the chamber, Aride placed the last sachel down on a bench just out side the door and walked away.

"Bye my brother" he whispered so not to be heard.

Sitting down on his throne for the first time, his

servent walked up to him. "You were right, he was intending to blow you up Cole". But Cole laughed as if his servent had told him a joke. "Leave quickly before it goes off, I need you to follow my steps".

The servent stayed away from the throne as it blew up, he covered him self as he grinned he knew that his master would forget about certain things once he was brought back from the dead. He waited in the center of the room, waiting out that last of the explosions. The door opened slightly, as the shadow looked back in fear, an explosion rocked the door clean off its hinges. A body fell foreward, "Noooo" he screamed. "Guards, guards come quick your master has been murdered".

Several shadows entered the room all of them shock by the display, it wasn't just Cole that died but his master as well.

"Who did this?" One of the shadows asked hoping to get a straight answer.

"It was Aride, Cole had his suspions about his brother. He intends to go after Gemmel". The servent said.

The Land of Waller

Into Danger They Go

It had taken them all the next day to get as far north they could get before twilight had fallen, the four of them had just reached a wooden area, just before the forest that waited for them which was on their left side. None of them knew that Gemmel wasn't there since it was the broken sword had been layer within the tower that stood in the center. One couldn't miss it since it lumbed over the forest many miles away. This area was unexplored and unmaped, its said that greater dangers lerked here. Reid had heard the tales but he dimissed them as children stories since he grew up listneing to them him self. Tucker had been here once before, he knew what to expect from the area.

"Careful" he cautioned as he pointed at a hidden hunter. The three watched the area trying to see what Tucker was pointing at. A single small bird landed on the ground to grab a worm that surfaced, it peakedat it suddenly a neearby tree grabbed the animal and opened its mouth. It ploped the dead bird into its mouth as it ate.

"…Holy shit…" Reid said with a start. He gazed at the creature not sure what it was. "that tree –

"That's not a tree" Tucker interrupted as he motioned them to watch further. Hair grew out from the bark, as roots were pulled in as a set of legs formed which were as big as a man. The four were breathless at the sight, Reid looked at Tucker in puzzlement and with horror. He had never seen anything like this before.

"What the hell is that thing?" he was dead serious since Reid needed to know.

"That is a Drago, a deadly changeling that can detect anything" Tucker paused seeing that his friends were amazed and terrified by the news.

"How did you know that?" Reid asked then changed his mind as he raised his hand. "On second thought, I rather not know.

Tucker breathed a sigh of releaf since he didn't have to tell his tale. Once this forset was beautiful long ago but now it was a thing of nightmares now. For five centuries, the Immortal Empire had ruled only to crumpled onto it self since an anicent evil had entered the city. Before it fell Tucker was born along with a few others. He had no choice to return to this nightmare forest, they needed the broken sword to defect Talin.

Moving forward once more, Tucker glanced back to see an abandoned old building, he remember it since he was only a child then. He yanked his head away trying to focus on the task at hand. His nightmare was becoming true, he had it a few nights ago but it was his own curse since he was an Immortal since they saw the future that would come to pass.

"We better settle for the night" Reid annouced but Tucker glanced back at him, he knew that they shouldn't even camp out in the open.

"Can't stay here" Tucker told the group since he was on edge. He glanced over both his shoulders expecting something to happen.

"Why can't we camp here?" Rachel asked concerned her Tucker since he was a friend. He looked right into her eyes as he breathed.

His eyes was terrified, all Tucker wanted to do was leave the forest but he knew that they needed that sword.

"You don't want to know" he answered sharply, he turned away from her as he eyed the nearby mountain that stood in their way.

"I take it you've been here once before" Bobby said but unsure if he should be asking the question in the first place. Tucker looked at his friends, unsure what to tell them.

"Fine" he started since he felt defeated by his own friends since they wanted answers to their questions. "No one comes here, not even for the broken sword". Tucker paused for a second. "People have tried to travel through this forest only to die in the attempt. The stories you heard when all of you were kids are true. Monsters of unexpected evil kill those that want the sword. the name sake messes with your head, it's not really broken". He paused to let the news sink into his friends of the horrors that they are about to face. "Before all this" Tucker continued "a great empire ruled these lands. This forest was beautiful once, it has been over a thousand years now. A great evil came and destoryed it, filling it with nightmare creatures that could kill you while you sleep".

Reid swallowed not liking the idea now, he now knew why Tucker didn't want to step into this forest in the first place. But something else was nagging at him, but he couldn't fathom why.

"Can you suggest where we should camp for the night?" Reid asled trying to keep his own anger down since the place was getting to him as well.

"A cave at the bottom of that mountain" Tucker

piped up. "It's the only place that's safe" he moved away from them as he lead them the way to the cave since he knew the area well. Tucker knew that he was being watched, he didn't care at all since he knew that his own people were watching him and his friends. Following the immortal, Rachel and Reid began to whisper to each other.

"There's something Tucker isn't telling us" Rachel began trying to keep her voice low enough so not to be heard.

"Leave it alone.. he seems disturbed" Reid cauntioned as he pointed at his friend. "Look at him, he's not the same Tucker that I know. Since we stepped in here he had been nervous and snappy" as he shook his head concerned for their friend.

"He's spooked" Bobby offered as the two looked

back at him.

"Spooked, he's more than spooked" Rachel spat out trying to understand why Tucker had volentered to lead them in the first place.

"Makes sence" Reid said as a bright light filled the night air, it stung their eyes since it got their attention.

"Tucker" Reid called out not sure what had happened to their companion, that stood frozen.

"Tuck" he said once more as he put his hand on his friends shoulder but Reid knew that his friend was frozen on the spot. Turning his head to the right a human like figure walked toward them.

"Who are you?And what have you done to me friend" Reid demanded.

" Need not be afraid travelers" the dark figure told them as it strolled up to them and the immortal.

"I thought I told you not to come back here …

Traitor". Reid stepped forward not liking this person right away.

"Release him, now" Reid threatened as he drew his sword.

"Or you'll what, butter me with that silly knife of yours" the figure in black said. Mocking the human and his ability with his sword.

"Kill you" Reid threatened once more as the sword came close to the immortal, but which didn't flinch at all.

The man started to laugh at the idea, amused by the human and his ability.

"You seek the broken sword" the man taunted them, as he curled his lips in hatred. This immortal hated all humans but he was intreged why his own brother had returned with these brothers.

"Yes, that's right. We seek the sword, Tucker didn't want to return at all. But at least he's willing to help us" Rachel replied as she lifted his hand hoping something would come out of this.

"Go to the cave for the night, come day break I suggest you go to the castle at the norht end of the mountain" he yoned and lead them to the hidden cave.

"Why should we trust you" Reid said distastefully as he sat down on the cave floor.

"You have no other choice… but I guess I should tell you why Tucker is spooked" the figure said not willing to give away his identity. The three leaned forward as they listened eagerly. "It's because of the Petals and me" the man said as he now lowered his hood.

Reid shifted his eyes, thinking of what they were.

Not sure what a Petal was, then he remembered the tales.

"Why would he be afraid of flowers" Rachel guessed, not sure her self but at least she tried to answer.

"No" Reid finally said " their an off shoot of the elves" but he stopped since the stranger looked pleased by the answer.

"It's the other way around, Petals were the first evil long ago. Then there was a war for over three hundred years, elves over took the lands, but it didn't last long ntil they found out that the first of the drow were born" the stranger told them, trying to help them but at the same time trying to make be afraid for once.

Reid looked satisfied with the tale, but he

interupted the strangers continue his story.

"Four other races were born as well, according to legend, but why did you have to freeze Tucker?" Reid wondered as he watched the man look at him for the first time.

"Had to since the Petals were about to attack" the stranger said feeling uncomfable by all this.

"So is this all about you as well" Reid asked hoping that the stranger would not harm him or his friends.

"Tucker had betrayed us long ago, to the Petals for that I had to banish my brother" the stranger said at last which surprised the group. The strangers eye's turned soft for once, they noticed a single tear ran down his cheek. "He" the stranger pointed at "was not allowed to return" he growled.

* * *

Sitting in a clearing not to far from the ruins of the

old elven town. Gemmel watched the dear eat the grass. It was several feet away but Linda knew what to do. She had told him not to move, for if he did the beautiful creature would bolt from the spot.

Wow, he mouthed and then noticed something different about Linda for the first time.

"Lin" he whispered. The dear looked up and stared at the human then slowly walked away.

"Yep" she replied as he looked at her closely .

"You look different, the last time I saw you" Gemmel exclaimed as he studied her from head to foot trying to see what it was. Was it her clothes, the stance she had or the perfume that smelled differently. Gemmel could not tell at all.

"I grew my hair" Linda said then noticed that he was studying her.

"That and something else" he replied not sure what the something else was since it puzzled him, but he watched her move. A slight glow of yellow could be seen around her, it was a hue of some accord.

"Your not human" Gemmel sputtered, caught off guard by his own surprise since he had never noticed it before.

"You just figured that out" Linda told him as she laughed heartedly, but he didn't look frightened at all, he was stunned.

"I'm one of the Bon Elves, the magic ones the humans call us. Some times humans or dwarves think us as the immortals, which isn't true at all. Tucker is an old immortal" she finished pointing out the difference.

"W-who's this Tucker" Gemmel woundered not sure what to make certain of his friend. "Is he an old boy friend".

She thought that over for a second, being careful to answer such a question but she knew that it must be answered.

"He's really just a friend of mine" Linda replied hoping that she didn't hurt his feelings.

"For several days now, I've been trying to figure out why I'm here, but no one answers me" Gemmel told her unsure if he were wrong in some way. She didn't know what to say at first since she had no idea what Corp has told the boy.

"Did he say anything to you" Linda questioned him, as he now leaned back onto an old wall.

"He said that he's trying to protect me from something, that I have no idea" Gemmel informed her as he looked confussed by something. He felt ashamed and quilty, but yet he had no idea why.

"Talin" she assured him, telling him who they were protecting him from. They only needed to tell him one side of the story but not all of it, Linda would never tell Gemmel that he used to be evil.

"There's that name again, I know that he's evil and all but why is he pursing me" Gemmel now paced the small area.

"It's not that simple" Linda replied calmly. She could tell that he was getting angry by the second.

"SO HE KILLED YOU FAMILY, WHAT HAS HE DONE TO ME…NOTHING, I TELL YOU" he looked shocked by his anger. As he watched her cry, tears ran down her cheeks, Linda remembered the day when Talin had killed her family.

"I" he replied, trying to appoligise for his out burst.

"He wants to use you as a tool, to destory

everything that we hold dear. Your own magic is buried within you, with that magic nothing can stop him" Linda informed her young friend as she cried at the memory. Gemmel looked shock by the news as he shook his head.

"An Orge wants me dead and Talin wants me alive. I need your help" Gemmel said as he paused so he could think.

"What are you suggesting?" she asked in wonderment.

"Help me bring the magic back within me" Gemmel pleaded as Linda blinked as a smile formed.

"Your learning all ready" Linda responded which caught him off guard. He looked perplexed at her not really understanding what she meant by it.

"What do you mean?" he wondered not noticing

the dear at all.

"That dear is about ten feet from us, dear never come that close" Linda pointed out trying to make him see. Again he looked puzzled as he thought about the encounter for the first time.

"I thought you did that" Gemmel said thunderstuck by the thought that he did it and not her. Linda shook her head, still smiling at him.

"You started using your magic since you discovered the ruins, I've only been helping you to reclaim your magic. Now, now it's time for you to learn to defend yourself if your going to survive a battle of any sort". Linda told him, but he felt that not all was told to him. She was holding back something and he now could sense it.

He smiled weakly at the thought. Now I will have power, Gemmel thought pleased by the out come. But before long the boy that was Gemmel will be no more. The two of them fought and trained during the days ahead, each burning off the extra fat that the two of them had. Then came the magic spells, each were draining but Gemmel had refueled quite quikely. It took time for Linda to refuel since she was slightly older than him.

"Now" Gemmel uttered to his lady friend as she let fly an arrow, he looked up at it as it got nearer and nearer to him. He put up an invisble shield just in time, as the two saw the arrow bounce off it.

"You did it" Linda said excitedly and patted him on the back and then hugged him for the first time. She started to pull back but he kissed her on the lips, Linda looked startled not sure why he had done it in the first place.

"At least it worked, but you know the drill if you don't get it right. Lets try something new, if you get the next four you will pass" Linda said trying to forget about the kiss.

"Don't you love me?" Gemmel asked not sure why Linda had pulled away from him. Watching her walk away from him, he cried out for her to stop. She turned toward him, arrow in one hand and the bow in the other. Linda didn't speak as she louded the bow. "Tell me that you love me" Gemmel pleaded.

An arrow came at him, the sheild came up hitting the arrow just in time. But she didn't stop, arrow after arrow came toward him. He started to walk to her, bringing his hand up stopping the arrows as they hit the small shield one after the other.

Gemmel got close to her, she stoped shooting the

arrows. "Don't you love me" he repeated as he saw her shed a tear.

"Yes, I do but I can't. It's hard to explain" Linda told him but he needed more than that. He leaned in hoping she would respond and she did.

He whirled around just in time, as an arrow headed toward them. He grabed it between his fingers. Gemmel looked at it, stunned by his sudden move. Looking up from the arrow he noticed Bracer for the first time.

"Leave Linda alone, kid. Her husband would kill you for touching her, besides I see your learning more. Sorry Linda, I had to make sure if his reflexes were a lot better" Bracer said as Gemmel felt like a fool for the first time. He turned to her stunned by the news.

"Your married, you should have told me. I fell in love with you" he turned away from her wanting to run off but something stopped him from doing so.

Gemmel felt betrayed, but Linda had stopped him before he made a scene. She walked toward him, and then stood in front of him as she studied his face. Linda could see the hurt on his face, she felt for him but she knew what it was like to love someone and be rejected by love.

" I'm sorry, Gemmel. Though in my defence, I never thought you would love me that way, Reid is my husband. He would kill you for just kissing me, but I know what it's like not to be loved by the person you think you love." Linda informed him as she smiled at him. "Besides I do love you as a friend". Which perked him up.

"It seems your ready to face that orge after all" Bracer informed the boy who now smiled back. Gemmel looked at her pleased to still have her as a friend.

"I guess I should appoligise for the way I was acting, I never thought that you were all ready taken" Gemmel said trying to push aside his feelings for her.

"Come then, we have a two day walk " the chief told him as they walked away, the human followed the elf. "We're pleased that you finished the map, we had forgotten how big our forest is, because of you the other tribes have been united so that we can protect this forest. The elves are returning to the lost city of Thornin, we are in your debt"' Bracer informed

him as Gemmel felt pleased that he had reunited the

elven tribes as he looked at the elf with pride.

After two days of travel to the edge of the forest, Gemmel looked at the spot where he had fallen two weeks ago. An elf let fly an arrow into the orge camp which killed one of them. The leader looked up from the dead body.

"Well, well" the leader snarled in hatered "let the games begin" he whispered harshly as the others of his tribe laughed at the thought.

Standing in the open field Gemmel's heart raced as he atched the leader gain up on him. The invisible wall went up which forced the beast back a few steps.

"Magic" the orge roared then began to circle the human trying to find a flaw in the humans attack but he couldn't see it at all. Gemmel remembered what Linda had shown him, the orge jumped and reached back with it's right arm. Insteadly the wall came back up forcing the orge to fly backwards.

He landed onto his back, but rolled over onto it's feet.

The orge wasn't pleased at all, anger fueled his strengh.

The beast walked back ten steps and began to run, Gemmel had no idea what was happening. He then felt fear for the first time, the elves started to yell at him in warning. His instinks took over, he pointed at the arrow without looking at it, it caught on fire and his invisibel wall sprang up just in time. The orge bounced back once again, stunned by the the force.

Gemmel reached out with his mind trying to take control of the arrow, the orge lunged at him. The fire arrow shot passed him only by a few feet, in beding it self into the heart of the orge. It dropped to the ground, fully dead.

The second in command could not believe his luck as he raced over to his dead leader. He stopped as he looked over his dead brother, he picked him up now staring at the human with hateful eye's.

" You got lucky human, I will kill you for what you've done" the orge snarled "but not today"' he told the human coldly.

Once back within the forest, Bracer smiled at the human male.

"You did a better job than I thought possible" Bracer told his human friend but Gemmel strolled away with his head hung, he hated killing the orge but he knew it had to be done. "Gemmel is something wrong?" Bracer asked concerned for the human but he knew something had hurt the boy.

"NO" Gemmel snapped angrily, he was still blaming himself for falling in love with Linda. He had poured his emtions into the fight and it worked, all he wanted to do now was cry. "Now I have to fight it's brother". Bracer placed his hand on the boys shoulder before he could go any where.

"Some times the fight brings anyone down. Even if they thought it was over. Still those Orges have no idea who you are" Bracer tried to help him. Gemmel shot the elf an evil look without meaning to.

"You have no idea of who I am Bracer. I don't even know my self, but for all we know I could be your enemy" Gemmel pointed out trying not to upset the elf. His eyes turned soft and went over to the campfire.

Linda strolled over to Bracer who looked toward her with a smile. He feared for the boy since they all knew the truth, but they kept it from him.

"I fear it my self, Bracer. I sure hope we can keep Gemmel good …this time".

Four

More than Enough

As the three set foot on the loose gravel by a river, Rachel wiped the sweat off her forehead. She looked around at the scene, trying to see the castle.

"Where is this castle?" she urged as she noticed Reid looking at something not sure what it was at first.

"I think that answers your question" Reid stated as he and Bobby smiled at the ruins.

"Come to Daddy" Bob said eagerly to get this done with. Rachel laughed at the thought, since she found it funny that Bob was eager to reach the goal.

"We traveled for two days to get here only to dicover that nothing is gurading this place at all" she babbled.

Reid studied the area with his two eyes, he sensed that there was something here and yet he couldn't see it.

"There is danger here" he insisted, he caught movement in the corner of his eye. Reid looked in the direction but he couldn't see anything at all.

"How would you know?" Rachel asked in wonderment, trying to stay calm but the forest had unnerved her.

"There's no animals but something is watching us, I can feel it" Reid voiced his fear as he surveyed the area trying to calm him self but yet he couldn't seem to at all. Linda nodded as did Bob, they all had the same feeling though they had no idea if it was evil or not. The three stayed rooted to the spot.

"We might as well set up camp" Reid announced as the three of them slowly unpacked for the night. All of them knew that they weren't going to get any sleep, since they were being watched.

Something moved in the corner of Rachels eye, she jumped, startled by the movement. Something flew passed her ear,just missing her.

"Aaaaahhhh" she yelled which caught Reids and Bobs attention. Shadows moved, as they looked up. Bob looked down for a second and saw a skull of some sort, it wasn't in his pack before.

"Something is trying to scare us away, Reid" Bob said as he picked up the skull, which oddly looked like a humans.

"Put that down, Bob. You don't know where your hands have been" Reid joked but his friends moaned by the slight attempt of humor. Going into his own pack, a snake wraped it self around his hand and arm.

Reid smiled at it, seeing that it was too frighten him but he wasn't a fraid of snakes at all. "Look at this, this little devil found a warm place to stay the night".

Rachel and Bob glanced toward him and saw the snake, they only grinned at the sight of the snake.

"We'll someone has no idea how to frighten you. If I were to try I would have put a rat in there" Bob tried not to grin since he was lying though his teeth.

"I hate rats" Rachel remarked as she shuddered at the thought. Something moved in her pack, moving away from her own pack. "Reid, Bob. Would either of you find out what's in there".

Both of them came over to help, Reid lifted the pack he could tell it was huge though not sure what it was. He tipped it, as everything came out even the animal, it wsn't a rat at all but a small chipmounk.

It nibbled on a nut, both men laughed at the sight

which lightened the mood.

"Someone is trying to get ride of us, but a snake and chipmounk won't frighten us away. You have to do better than that, who ever you are" Reid called out into the forest.

As the sun crested the horizen the following morning, the three felt refreashed from the night before. The pranks had stopped, but still they felt they were being watched. All three of them stood infront of the entrance of the old castle.

"Fox" Rachel read out loud, but Reid could tell that the over growth had covered half the sign. Shifting it away the rest of the sign could now be read.

"Dead Fox" Bob said out loud as Reid finished moving the brush away.

"What a name, though I think there's another word

in there somewhere" Bob pointed out as Reid nodded as he went back to work. It did indeed have a third word but not one that they would have picked. All of them read the sign which was very strange to look at.

"Dead Fox Castle" all of them read as Reid shook his head, trying to understand the name but couldn't.

"We might as well enter" Bob piped up and started for the door.

"Wait" Rachel shouted in alarm, but a tree branch shot out of the forest nocking Bob to the ground.

People dropped from the trees all armed with swords. One of the men held his own sword at Bob, who looked up at him.

"Any last words" a voice said to the three.

Reid thought for a moment, trying to see what he should say but found him self saying out loud.

"B-Broken Sword" Reid said trying to see if it

worked or not. Swords eased back, but Reid needed to know who spoke to them.

"Turn around slowly" a voice told them, Reid and Rachel did as they were told to do. Facing their unknown attackers who were masked, one of them with drew his mask. Rachel's mouth dropped open, stunned by the sudden appearance.

"Ruban Elves" Rachel excalimed more in shock than being calm. His silvery long hair, blew in the wind as he moved closer to them.

"You've heared of us, mage" the elf said.

"I'm a druid, not a mage" Rachel pointed out trying to be calm and collective in her manner.

"Sorry about the scare last night… I'm Athen and these are my comrades" as he looked at the small group. "Why are you Seeking the broken sword?"

Athen asked as Bob got to his feet at last.

"To defeat Talin" Reid announced as the elf held his gaze on the human male, the swords were put away.

"Only a true King can defeat Talin with the sword, if you are that person we will let you enter. But beware, danger lurks in that ancient building" Athen turned to leave with his comrades, they slowly disappeared from sight.

"Wait" Rachel called out as the elf stopped in mid stride. "How can we get in?" she wondered as he winked back at them then left the area.

"Great, just great. I can't believe he likes you" Reid grinned at the thought but Bob had looked back at the building.

"He didn't … the door is wide open" Bobby cheered with delight. Rachel looked back at the direction the elves had left then looked at the open door, she smiled as she shook her head.

"What's wrong" Reid asked as he studied her.

"I thought the wink was for me, I never thought it was for the door" Rachel said as she moved to the open door, with Reid following behind.

"Boy, it's really musty in here" then sniffed the air as Bob blinked his eyes. "What's that smell?" he had to ask trying not to guess what it might be.

" It wasn't me" Reid said as he held his nose and covered his mouth at the same time trying no to gag or throw up at the stench. A skeleton was on the floor a few feet from them. "Does that answer your question".

Rachel stopped a second later and held out her hand to stop the two of them.

"Something wrong" Reid said as she picked up

some dust which she threw ahead of them. Red lights lined the scattered around the floor, it wasn't possible to cross since they were so close togther.

"What in the name are those" Bob questioned not liking the look of the red lights at all. He dropped his soak that was in his hand, it fell onto the red line line only to see it disappear.

"Old magic" Rachel said "some one set up traps to keep people out of here" she told them as she thought for a moment.

"Can't we go around it?" Reid suggested.

"No" she replied.

"Since we can't walk can we floot over them" Bob suggested, then thought better at it since he had was sick to his stomach the last time they had to floot over a huge hole once. Reid looked at his friend and smiled warmly.

"You could stay here and stand guard" Reid suggested but Bob shook his head not liking the idea of being separated at all.

"I won't leave you" Bob answered back as Rachel now laughed.

"At least Reid distracted you" Rachel pointed out.

"What do you mean?" Bob wondered not knowing what was going on as Reid patted him on the back.

"We're on the other side buddy" Reid said as he pointed at the location where they stood before.

Glade that he didn't throw up, Bobby followed his friends, as the rounded a corner half an hour later Reid jerked his friend back just in time. Huge blades, swung out of the walls, Rachel studied them with horror on her face.

"Thank God, Reid pulled you back in time" Rachel

said but noticed that Bob had been sick.

"Let the druid do the leading, Bob" Reid said with a grin as he noticed a door just to their right.

Five

A Deeper Threat

Aride stood over looking a cliff, the view of the land scape filled his vision. He enjoyed the sight all to well, the leaves and grass and the trees filled his sences. Nothing compared to the lush surrounding that he enjoyed so much, his thoughts were on his brother. The way he was treated with little regard, Cole was never one to support his on family.

"Aride" a voice said from behind him. He didn't even look over his shoulder, he just stood there trying to focus on the sight.

"Yes" Aride responded, in a rough voice. "What do you need me to do?" he asked suspiously.

"We must prevent Gemmel from reaching his goal. You know of this… It's what we intend to do. He's trying to come to turms, even if he lost his memory" the voice said, still Aride didn't turn around. But he pondered the words, he knew that they were true.

"I"ll send out some troops to deal with him. Even if he doesn't remember a thing, he still is a threat to me" Aride said slightly agicated from the very thought.

"What troops have you thought should go out? There are more than enough orc's or rock trolls to command sir." The small gnome said, now seeing his master turn around for the first time. Aride looked down at him, he had an idea that he was considering.

"Send out some trolls and Orc's, but only one I can think of can help rid me of my problem. Send Ston as well". Aride remarked, his eyes lite up in glee at the thought.

Nothing could stop Ston unless, he was over powered but he was more than needed. The gnome just looked up at him, his mouth hung open in shock. He hated to deal with such a powerful entity, Ston, the gnome thought with pure distaste. Turning away from his master, he cursed under his breath. The notion of talking to him made him sick. Leaving the vast chamber, he turned right. A leg stopped him from moving.

"Watch it, gnome" the Orc snapped a bit to hastly. The gnome looked up and smiled weakly, seeing the half breed known as Ston.

"Arid wishes for you to join a search" the small gnome said but the half breed glared down at him.

"I take no commands from such as you" Ston threatened, bending his weapon. The gnome gulped, now fearful that Ston might do the same thing to him. "I take orders from Aride only not some half whit like you" Ston said disgraced at such a thought. He held his head high, looking down his nose at any who didn't measure up to his standards. He marched into Arides room, with the gnome on his heals pleading him to listen to him.

"Ston" Aride said, wondering why he had appeared in his chambers. "Why are you still here?" he growled slightly angry at the commander.

"As I was telling this gnome I take orders from you only sir" Ston said with disguse, upset with the gnome for nothing than a simple order.

"You should have listened to him Ston. I gave him the order to tell you, do this one more time and I'll get the Flours on you" Aride now threatened the Orc with open hatred. The Orc growled deeply, his eyes light up ready to take on his master.

"I will not listen to gnomes, they are short and have no idea how to fight. " Ston insisted, insulting the gnome right away without even thinking of it.

"Leave now" Aride growled for once more than displeased with the situation. He turned away, rolling his eyes. Ston just stood there dumbfounded, he glared down at the gnome with mock hatred .

"When I return with your prize, I want to see this gnome dead and his head on a spike" Ston now sounded amused by his own idea.

His master didn't like the sound to it, he glanced over his shoulder to see the Orc leave. Red eyes glowed, his mouth was in a snarl, much like a wild dogs. The gnome stayed at his side, hoping that the threat would not happen to him.

"You wouldn't let him kill me would you" the gnome asked, since he was looking up at his master. Aride gazed down, his expression softened a little but not by much.

"You are safe for now, I'll deal with him when he returns. Ston has been in my side since day one, this death threat is the last one he'll make" Aride said, releaving the gnomes fears. He gestered with his left hand indecating that he needed to be alone, the very nature of his being sparked like a growing flame. His eye's light up with pure hatered toward Ston since he had mostly upset him. The gnome left, not willing to be around his master, it sensed that his master was about to do some magic.

Aaahhh, sounded through out the lair, causing more than enough of Arides followers to look up from their work. Some turned their heads at the sound, whiping their human or elf slaves or whoever tried to escape. Aride closed his eyes feeling drained, from the out pour of emotion. Slumping against a wall, he noticed that he wasn't alone any more.

"Who the hell are you and why are you bugging me" Aride said turning around to see who had entered his chamber. He gazed at the single vampire that wore nothing but black.

"I maybe able to help out a little" the vampire said, feeling the coldness of the room. Just gazing at the empty walls which suited him just fine since he had served with many Tyrants over the past thousand years. Some of them had a much colder version, but this one was warmer than most.

"What kind of help? I seek only one thing and that is a boy that needs to die a painful death. He served with Talon some time ago and I intend to get rid of him. My brother can't stop me, not even the councel and yet they try to stop me at every turn." Aride thought for a moment, a small playful smile etched onto his face. The Shadow now beamed at the thought. “I might have something for you to do after all, they’ll get a bang out of it”.

“What are you talking about Aride? What ever it is might get you in trouble” Todd remarked, with his feet not even touching the floor.

“Your right about that Todd, but I have all ways liked to live that way. Besides with all the chaos, I might be able to finish up some things that I have been leaving unfinished” Aride said with a gleam in his eye.

\+ \+ \+

Ston stepped out into the open meadow, taking a breath of the clean air. Has gasped at it since he was accustemed to the smell of Orc and gnome oders. He glanced over his shoulder, seeing the enterence to the lair that he had come from.

A patrol of Orc's and Orgs stood before him, waiting eagerly for his orders. None spoke as he studied each and every one of them, two of his men looked injured but he didn't care.

"We have been given orders to find Gemmel. I want every single one of you to gather as much information as you can. Torture and kill as many humans you can, we need Gemmel alive, but who ever discovers the where abouts of such person will be rewarded." Ston stated with more than enough determination, his eyes glowed white enjoying the moment. Seeing his troops glance at each other, eager to help out as much as possible.

The Tyranny of Talin

"But who ever fails will die by my sword" Ston now threatened openly since he was toying with them.

"Boss, where should we look first?" an org said which was slightly bigger in nature to their cousins. Ston stared at the org, his face was hard and set, but it softened since he knew it was only a question.

"Try the farms first, don't kill the animals though. If I hear one of you did, I will gut you" Ston threatened them once again unhappy with the assignment.

Turning around he gazed up at the mountain, his thoughts filled with bitter hatered toward Aride. His soldiers disbanded, scattering into the field toward their intended goal.

"There's something wrong isn't there, boss. I take it Aride may have over stepped his boundry with you" another Orc said as Ston turned to look at his old friend.

"He pushes to hard, one day he may find himself at the end of my sword" Ston informed his Orc companion, which the thought pleased him more than was necessary. The orc just stared at him, not liking the sound to what Ston was impling and yet he knew that he should report to Aride about it.

"I have things to do" the orc said to him, brushing off an ant from his shoulder. Turning around, it went to the enterance of the lair.

Ston smiled, all knowning of what was about to go down. Perfect, he thought now scratching his chin as he pondered of what to do next. A warm breaze hit him in the face, breathing it in he wingled his toes feeling the softness of the grass. I really hate grass, he thought, strolling away from the lair. Heading toward a village that he actually knew about, once passed the the first field, he looked from side to side hoping that he wasn't being followed.

A shadowy movement caught his attention within the forest since he had looked back. Stopping to rest for a moment, Ston took a single breath as an arrow wized by him.

"Don't move Orc" an Elf said from behind him. Ston didn't move an inch, hoping that the single elf would be alone. Four arrows pointed at him, of which he had no clue.

"So it was you that was watching me from the forest" Ston replied, growling under his breath a second later.

The silver shoulder lengh hair hung loosely, just covering the elf's ears as he walked around the still figure. His angler features sparkled in the sunlight, enjoying this moment of tryumpth.

"Why are you out here? And are you looking for Gemmel" the nameless elf asked carefully, showing no emotion to the orc at all.

"How did you know that we were looking for Gemmel? And who tipped you off" Ston asked bluntly, narrowing his eyelides suspicionaly.

"I sent a scout ahead, he told me of your command and what you had to do. We are here to stop you from finding him at any cost" The Elf now threatened, keeping his bow and arrow up just in case the Orc rushed him.

"I seek him for only Arides sake, he wants him for some reason. All I know elf is that you better let me go before I kill you, your arrows will not kill me nor your strengh of will. Leave me now" Ston threatened openly, spitting at the ground in distaste.

Five more Elves stocked out into the open, their long swords glistened in the morning light as they surround the lone Orc. He seized up the five new elves, turning around carefully so not to get shot.

"Ten to one, I do like challenges" Ston smirked with more than enough pride, over confident in his own skills as a warrior.

"You shouldn't takes us all on, Orc. It could be your downfall, besides you have that mission" the same elf said pleasently, smoothing Stons temper.

Ston blinked, growing tired all of a sudden, he fought with all his will to keep his eyes open. Must not let them win, he thought as he closed his eyes. The elves watched him fall asleep, hands caught him , helping the body to the ground.

"We better get them all together, we must try to

find a way to control them before something happens" one of the male elves said, which seemed concerned for the Orc.

Placing their weapons away, three of the elves picked up the Orc, placing him down on a wooden strecher, which to of them pulled. They glanced around them as they journed through the field, making sure none of the flowers were disturbed.

Once on the edge of another forest, they unloaded the Orc making him lay there on the ground beside his own comrades.

"We better leave" one of the elves said. "They will wake in forty minutes, might as well tire them up now before they try something foolish".

"Your right, we must keep them like this for some time. Talin will make sure, that they don't bother us or him for quite some time" their commander said, disgrunted that they were still working for such a fowl traitor.

Rogon glanced at his troops as they tired up the Orc's he suspected that something wasn't right about the way his men was working. Uneasy about his subcommander since he suspected that he was spying for Talin. Standing guard along with two others, he instructed the rest to spread out to find any more that may have gone unnoticed.

Rogon just eyed his subcommander, not givening him a chance to kill him. Someone tapped him on the shoulder, turning slightly to see who it was, his mouth hung open in shock. The orc's stood behind him, two of his men held their swords. Their eye's looked red, he turned to look at his subcommander.

"You did this didn't you" Rogon accused him right

away. Seeing his subcommander go stiff in fright, but two of his men only laughed.

"I did not do this sir, I had suspected that these two up up to something" the subcommander said, looking upset at the thought.

"You will not get out easily" Ston said with gratitude, smiling in triumph over his own luck. "Your men are my men, except for the two of you. Leave before I decide to kill both of you".

"You think you have won Ston, I will get more elves and deal with you. Either that or I will warn them that you are coming to get Gemmel, we will not let Gemmel realize that he is part of Talin's schemes. He will be part of us once more, secondly your trespassing onto Elf territory, that is an act of war." Rogon informed Ston who looked him sternly in the face.

"My men have been trespassing for years Rogon, we see no truse. Now begon before I kill you and your tiny pup" Ston threatened, seeing the two head strong elves slowly back up. He waited until they were gone from sight, as he smirked once more.

"What are we going to do? Ston threatens us and our own men have turned on us. This is a bad sign, Rogon, and I don't like it" Merole said as he glanced over at his commander, marching back toward the far forest where Gemmel and the others of their tribe were hidden.

"There is something you don't know Subcommander and I better explain before you answer. The two that freed the Orc's are my own agents, I asked them to side with the others" Rogon said as Merole glanced at him in surprise .

"Nice, I never thought you knew about them. I bet you suspected I was in on it, truth is I was for a month. I just couldn't deal with all the lying and the spying, that's why I returned to our people. I asked our chief to drop the false charges" Merole remarked, remembering his painful time in Talin's lair.

"What happened in there? I suspect Talin tortured you as well" Rogon asked as they got a little closer to the forest which was a few hours away.

"It was worse than you think, I was carved up for two weeks. He intended to make me a Shadow like the rest of them, it just didn't happen. I may have done some bad things in the past but for some reason, I just didn't turn" Merole said ashamed at what he had done over the years. Tears came down his cheek, still feeling the sting of the sharp needles in the base of his back.

Rogon glanced at the elf's back seeing some blood on the base but not a lot. Lifting the shirt a little, he noticed several pin pricks where the needles had puntured the base of the elf's back.

"Your wound hasn't healed much, we better get back fast before you faint" Rogon said with concern, spotting a bird fly over to them. He smiled at once, reconizing the Roc right away. It landed infront of them glad to see them as well.

"Corp, we need to get back quick. Meroles wounds have opened once again, and the plan is going well" Rogon stated as the Roc nodded with approvel.

"Good, climb on board. I'll take you to your people" Corp answered gladly hoping there was time to talk over some matters. Climbing on the back of the Roc the two looked down as Corp jumped into the air, a current of wind carried them as they rose into the sky. The landscape marveled them as they watched several deer scatter below them.

A bear could be seen drinking from a river, and to its side lay a fish. An edge of a forest, loomed below them as they now decended, what might have been two hours walk turned into five minutes of air time. Landing just on the edge of a village, Corp changed into his elven half.

"Corp why are you back so soon? I wasn't expecting you back until later today" Bracer said as he looked at the two elves that looked as if something went wrong. "Was the mission a success?"

"Ston fell for it, sir. He thinks all of them are taitors, even the two we planted in his minst" Rogon informed him as one of the other elves took a look at

Merols wounds. Both walked away, as Bracer stared at his most trusted commander.

"Good, at least they will delay them for some time." He turned slightly to Corp and added. "Assemble the rest of my race, but take your time with it. We don't need you hurt since they live in another forest. Were you able to assign Reid and his companions to throw them off Gemmels involvement".

"I did sometime ago sir, I was able to convince them to retreave an ancent sword."

"This is sounding much better by the second, at least they must not know what's going on. Besides I fear the human race maybe attacked in the future, but I do fear that Two Swords maybe defeated" Bracer commented, concerned for the human village.

"I have to leave sir, we have to be more than

prepared for the coming war. " Corp remarked seeing his old friend nod in agreement. Turning away, he ran off toward the trees, jumping into the air he changed back into the giant bird, letting out a screach in excetment.

Shaking his head, Bracer smiled warmly as a single female strolled up to him. Turning around his eyes met hers, her red hair glistened in the sunlight, as she smiled at him.

"Gemmel is improving with his magic sir, but he's trying to hard to release all of his power." Linda commented, watching his blue eyes shine for a second.

"Slow him down, he must not fully embrace all of his power. Gemmel is recovering, I just hope he'll be able to stay on our side for once" Bracer said slightly concerned for the young man, as he thought about his own life as well.

"I hear your concern sir, it's just he's doing it on his own. Don't forget that he is older than he looks and drawing in that power once more may bring back over a hundred years of memory's, he may even remember who his fahter is as well" Linda stated, brushing aside some of her hair.

"We don't even know who his father is either, that we have to find out and fast. I just hope it's not someone we know and fear, besides we have other worry's at the moment. Just do what you can for Gemmel and keep an eye on him, just don't fall in love with him." Bracer spoke his inner thoughts on the matter as he considered his next words.

"I'll try my best sir, but it's not going to be easy at all since Gemmel has his own mind." Linda pointed out, moving toward the trees hoping that Gemmel wasn't too afraid to be left alone for too long.

Six

More than Enough Danger

They stood frozen on the spot, waiting out the the breaze. Ice formed, on their noses as they just stood there and yet, Reid knew that they had to move to keep warm. The corridor twisted and turned, ever so slowly they inched forward, a short sharp gasp of cold hurt his lungs from the bitter cold, but it didn't stop him. He was determined to get to the other side, he risked a look back at his two friends.

"This is too c c cold for me" Rachel gasped, agonizing over her covered hands, they were forced to wear thick furs which helped some what but they ploded on.

"We won't be able to make it" Reid shouted over the roaring wind which blasted at his face. He coughed, tying to get his breath back, inhaling he found that his teeth hurt. Must be from the cold, he thought as he took another step, a panel of floor gave way, exposing some heat from below. It warmed him slightly but not enough to help him.

"We have something new" he shouted over the rush of the wind, trying to locate where it was coming from. It puzzled him since they were in a ruined building, who had built this place and for what purpose he thought as he continued. Several more panels fell into the pit below, making the three a little warmer than before.

Something bubbled under them, causing some of the floor to melt. He looked over the edge, seeing magma flow under them.

"Ah hell" Reid gasped in triumpth, watching the flow of magma dift under them.

"Why stop now" Rachel asked, concerned for Reid since he looked back once more. His face was pale, she knew something was wrong right away.

"Magma" he called back, feeling the heat collide with his skin, but the cold wind helped to keep him safe for now.

Bob gazed at Rachel unsure what magma meant since he had never heard of it. He searched his memory just in case, since he didn't want to look like a fool for asking such a question.

"Just jump the gap" Rachel shouted, hoping that Reid could hear him.

He looked down at the small gap which was only three feet, stepping over it he felt releaved that part of the danger was gone for now. Looking down at the floor once more, he could smell something burn.

His eye's went wide in panic, he rushed foreward toward the cold snow that he had noticed, which seemed out of place.

"Where are we Rachel? This doesn't seem normal to me" as Bob agreed with his old friend.

"We're lost Reid, I think we entered a different realm unless this is all some sort of trap. My senses are telling me that there is magic all around us, this place has me as confused as you are." Reid rolled his eyes, as he stepped into the soft snow which cooled his shoes.

"This is odd" Bob stated unsure about this situation as well. He hated it when things didn't go right, nor when things went right, in either case they would figure it out and fast.

Reid gazed at the souls of his shoes, they didn't look as if they had melted at all. He gazed up at his two friends, puzzled since nothing seemed right.

"I think someone has been playing with us" Reid

said as he noticed a shadow move in the corner of his eye. He didn't dare to look in the direction since it might tip off who ever it was.

"At least we're out of danger at the moment as long as we stay put for a little while" Bob remarked with a sigh, not willing to take another step. A dart flew in the air toward him, Reid pushed him out of the way just in time. It struck an invisible wall, which all three looked surprised.

"Someone is testing us" Reid hissed, more than upset with the situation than he was letting on. Rachel patted the wall, testing it to see if there was some kind of door that would get them out of the corridor. She felt a door knob which crumbled by her touch, the door fell forward hitting the floor hard which set off a hidden trap as several darts lauched forward as they hit a nearby wall.

Rachel looked over her shoulder, glad that she wasn't in the room when the trap was triggered. She gazed into Reid's eyes studying the hard set face, Rachel could tell that he was trying his best to stay calm.

"Thank Eddings none of us were in there, we might have become pin cushions by now" Bob declaired, smirking at his own little joke.

Brushing his fingers through his hair, Reid sighed with releaf shaking off the uneasyness of his terrible fright. Heights trouble him but when it came to falling he cared nothing less about it, and yet he looked back passed the dart trap and into the tunnel of where he had his fright. Swallowing, he turned his attention back to his friends.

"Yes Bob, we did get the point… but I suspect there is more than what is going on. Someone doesn't want us in here and I need to find out why that Immortal needs our friend" Reid pointed out as he was concerned for his Immortal friend. The responciblity weighed heavly on him, he slumped for a second frightened of what the mysterous finger might do to them.

Tucker stared at his brother, he couldn't say a thing since he was frozen. His older brother just glared at him, since he was seated on a nearby rock.

"You should not have left us brother. I know you can't talk nor move but I don't care what you can do, we had to banish you for your own good. You know the real truth of the matter, you have suspected that it was me. Yes, it was" the other Immortal said now laying back just taking in the scene as he waited for the companions to return.

Tuckers hand moved slightly unbenouced to his own

brother since he looked into the forest, wondering if the humans had encountered the Ruben elves. "I suspect your friends may be dead brother, Ruben elves don't take prisoners".

Tucker shook trying to cast off the frozen spell, he fought harder, then relaxed falling into calmness to stay alert. He willed him self to fight, angry at his brother for showing his face. His inner laugh, caught the attention of nightmarish creatures that were sencitve to powerful magic.

You hear that brother, they are coming for you and when they find you here with me. The ruben elves will torture you.

His eyes stayed where they were, seeing movement ahead of them. He wanted to smile since he noticed several elves were hidden from sight, but being frozen had its advantages.

The elves glanced at each other now knowing the truth about the fallen empire. They looked shocked, anger filled their being at being betrayed by an Immortal that they had worshiped for countless centuries.

A single elf stared at the frozen Immortal, trying to communicate to him without trying to speak out loud. They didn't want the other brother to hear him, as the elf relaxed.

It looks like your brother has taken you hostage, I assure you we will punish him for what he has done to you. I can't believe he lied to us all this time, we'll get you out of this, the elf thought sending out the message.

You don't know the half of it, Rein not only has betrayed you but all of us. You need to kill him, his spell would be gone so that I could walk around once more. Not all of us are dead, several hundred of us Immortals have survived, I know this because I have encountered them over the past hundred years.

Tucker tried to blink but found that he couldn't, his frozen features looked soft and calm but it was his eyes that gave him away.

Anger spilled out, as he focused onto his inner thoughts trying to brush off the magic spell that he was under. His hand moved again but Rein didn't notice since he was way too busy looking another way.

'You could never escape little brother, so many centuries has softened you and being around humans has changed you too much. Look at what you've become, our empire maybe dead but we have survived. ' Rein turned slightly, ownly to be sucker punched.

"That's for being a traitor" Tucker snapped, as the ruben elves now surrounded them. Pure plain horror etched on their faces, determined to capture the traitor as Tucker stood over his fallen brother.

"Today and for the rest of my life, you're no longer my brother Rein. You caused our empire to fall, now suffer the concenquences." Tucker said, pained by the very betrail that his own flesh and blood had done to him.

Hands picked the fallen Immortal up to his feet as Rein gazed in puzzlement. His mind raced, trying to understand how his brother was able to defeat his magic spell.

"Not possible, none have been able to break the spell" Rein stated, being ushered into the forest by the ruben elves. Seeing Tucker smile back at him, as he was lead around some bushes. "One day I will kill you brother"

Standing on the boulder a second later, Tucker glanced down at the forest ground which was covered in leaves. The thought of his brothers betrail, now haunted him, as he sat down. Beside him was an elf, both were grime faced but the leader just didn't know what to say to ease the Immortals mind.

"You will have to return to deal with this threat Tucker. We can't hold Rein forever… besides I understand what your're going through at the moment. This effects us more than anyone of us can think of, you must stop Talin, he must not gain our country… nor become our ruler" the ruben elf said, sencing the Immortal was glancing at him.

The Tyranny of Talin

The Land of Waller
Seven

Too Many Evil Men

Pacing his own floor, Aride glance up at the vampire that entired his chamber. The white face showed no emotion what so ever as he walked up to him.

"Sir, I just found out that Ston has regained control on the elf traitors but he is still looking for the boy. One of them has seen the boy on the distant side of Waller, just near the human city of Fant. He has sent three of his men to investigate the matter" the vampire informed his boss as Aride looked away from him.

"It's a foolish mission, tell Ston to kill the elves, all of them are spies" Aride announced.

"Spies, you must be wrong. They freed the Orc's and everything" the vampire insisted, trying not to show any emotion.

"I assure you that they have not turned their backs on their own cause. It's how elves think fool, I should know I was once an Elf as was my brother Cole" Aride said with bitter taste at the long memory. He just glared back angirly, wishing to hurt the vampire but he backed off, just incase the vampire decided to fight back.

"Ston will get what he deserves" the vampire implied with a smirk as he schemed with his master. Aride approved of the vampires suggestion but first he needed the boy, the young yelp that had endangered his own mission. Turning away from his vampire friend, Aride took a few steps forward as he tried to think of what to do in the coming days. And for some reason everything that he held dear was coming into play, the way he wanted. The smirk on his face told the vampire so.

"We must prepare for the coming strike. Our leaders will suspect our enemy will be behind the attack" Aride finally said, as his eye's sparkled with glee.

Eight

In heap of trouble

Leaning on the stone wall, Reid had his eyes closed thanking to Eddings that he had survived the last trap. His two dear friends stood near him, breathing hard since they were nearly pined by needles.

"I rather not go back that way" Bob declaired sighing with releaf, frightened of what might happen next. His torch went out, making it darker for them to see where they needed to go but Reid wasn't all that worried about it.

"Just watch your stepping, I rather not go through another trap. Now light that torch again, I can barily see you or Rachel" sounding upset with the situation. Seeing the torch light up once more, Reid half grined, but he ignored the pain in his leg. Glancing down at his right leg, he noticed several pins in the back of his lower leg.

"You're hurt" Rachel said in symperthy, bending down to tack a better look at it. "Bring the torch closer" she instructed seeing the aweful wound. Bob tock a few steps closer, lowering the torch but not to close, he gasped then cringed at the sight. Watching her taking out the pins, Reid cringed in pain everytime she took another one out. Tears ran down his face, forcing himself not to collaspe nor faint.

"I done" she finally said, glad that he was out of danger just as she ran her hand over his wound which vanished a second later.
Releaf dawned on him, making him feel better but the

grim hope faded as he looked off into the darkness of the ancient ruins.

Nine

A horrable thing happens

Stepping into the dark room, Aride glanced at the others of his kind which were talking in a deep converation. Several of the counsil members was sitting in the room just on the other side of the table, a friend of his looked up and saw him. She was closer to him, her shoulder lengh dark hair moved slightly since she was walking over to him.

"Why are you here, Aride?" a mighty voice rang out but the shadow hid his snear.

"I come with grave news" Aride told the counsel trying to think what to say to them.

"What is it?" one of the cousel members asked

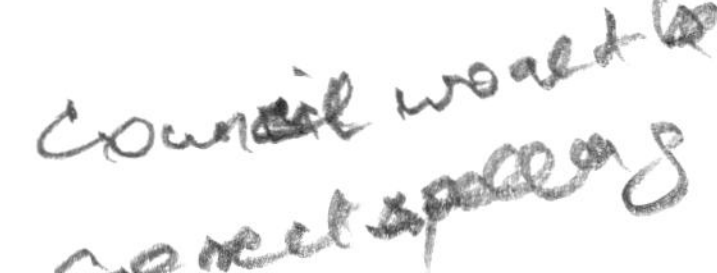

slightly impatient with the shadow, he got up from his chair and leaned on the table. He wasn't pleased to see a non member in the room, his head was bald and at fill hieght was only six feet tall.

"My brother has been killed" Aride announced to the counsel, everyone of them looked at each other surprised by the news, Except the bald man that leaned on the table, which glared at him hatefully.

"Killed you say, who would do this and why?" another figure asked.

"It was Talin" Aride whispered harshly, but none of them looked surprised. Each and every member of the counsel knew that they were marked for death. Some were prepared to die as others had casted spells from dieing.

"He has been in our back side for too long" a

cloaked figure said as he then pointed his arm toward the door. "Leave us" he ordered.

Waiting for Aride to leave the counsel room, the members watched him leave the room.

"Drako" a familier voice said "do you believe him" but the bald man shook his head.

"I don't , I believe he killed his brother" Drako spat out with mock haterid as he watched a shadow emerge into the room. The counsel looked up to see the figure, all of them looked surprised to see the face of the shadow.

"We thought you dead" Drako said with surprise within his voice. Cole looked at his friends before he spoke, studying them with his scanful eye's.

"I had casted a spell to prevent my death, it was to

make my enemies think I was truly dead" he paused for a moment, letting it sink in for the counsel. "I must leave here to deal with Talin" Cole remarked as he turned to leave. "Aride will find a way to kill each and every one of you" he warned as he approched the door.

Drako smiled as did the rest of the cousel.

"We always plan ahead" Drako shouted as he watched the shadow walk way. Leaving the chamber Cole noticed the small package. He knew who planted it, he launched a magic bubble at it which consumed it.

"Boom" then another one went off just on the other side of the counsel chamber. Aride hide within the shadows with a smile on his face, a figure stepped up to him from behind. Strong hands grabbed onto him, which turned him around.

"Who are you?" Aride demanded struggling, trying to escape from the powerful hands. He then noticed the counsel looking at him for the first time.

"What's going on, I thought you all died" Aride looked surprised, as he tired to get free once again but hands had him.

"I see" a familier voice said, Aride looked up at the figure for the first time. His face went pale, now knowing that his game was now up.

"Cole" Aride said fearful for his life. "How did you survive?".

"That's unimportant" his brother said then leaned close to him. Cole looked more than upset, he was angry by his brothers actions. "Guard's take him away".

Drako strolled up to the shadow, his face was more

in a snarl then his own brothers. Aride had no idea what was about to happen.

"I um ma" Drako uttered for all to hear, surprise filled Arides face.

"NOOOOO" he screamed as his magic was drained from him, his body convalsed. Every fibre in him fought off the spell, but he was losing his magic at a ramped speed. Aride lay on the floor for a second, he panted heavily. The bald shadow looked at the once shadow, who was now an elf.

"Return this traitor where he came from" Drako ordered. As several of the guards picked up the elf, some of them hit him as others spat toward the traitor, as the group of guards was escorting him out of the building.

* * *

Searching through his room, Talin grabbed the

object that he was looking for. It's silvery surfice spakled in the sun light, which didn't bother the elf at all.

"Linda" he whispered then noticed that he wasn't alone. "B'Jorn" he said in surprise to see his third commander.

"Bad news sir, Gemmel is now using magic" B'Jorn said, he noticed that his boss wasn't pleased by the news and nor should he. Talin wasn't surprised at all but he was shooked to learn about it.

"Anything else, I should know about" Talin demanded as he looked at the drow.

"He's killed one of our commanders" the drow informed him, slightly backing up from his boss.

Talin looked as if he were about to launch a fit of some sort, but he kept it bottled up for the moment.

Though Talin started to laugh at the idea, he knew that Gemmel would regain his memory.

"He will be mine once again" Talin assured his commander, which looked puzzled at the thought.

"Sir" B'Jorn said not sure what he was hearing, still puzzled over the whole thing. "Who are you referring to" the drow wondered.

Talin glared at the drow, his lips were tight together. He wasn't in the mood for such questions.

"Leave me" Talin urged his commander as the drow turned away, he watched the drow commander leave the chamber. Looking in his ahnd that held the silver object, he now squeezed it tightly. "Linda must be helping the boy". Talin said coldly as he turned to see another figure enter the chamber.

"Cole" Talin said with surprise as he heard his own voice chock. He cleared his throat before he spoke to his own boss. "What took you so long?" he asked.

"Nothing to concern your self, is the plan going as planned" the shadow asked the elf who looked back at him.

"One of my captain's died" Talin informed him.

"Pity" Cole said with a cold smile "Is Gemmel here yet" Cole wondered hoping that he wasn't.
He sensed that Talin was getting angry at the thought, Cole took pleaser in it.

"Does it look like it" Talin said sarcasticaly, but the shadow noticed the silver object in the elf's hand.
Cole reconized the ring but he couldn't place where he had seen it before.

"I take it you're remembering a forgotten love"
Cole now remembered where he had seen the ring

once before as he looked Talin up and down.

"Linda is planning something" he replied coldly.

"She might turn him to the light" suggested Cole as he sat down on a chair that stood to his right. "Besides it does't matter. He will die either way".

Talin was getting angry all over again, he gave him a sharp cold look.

"I need him alive" Talin roared as he watched Cole was making himself at home. "What are you doing?" he snarled, truly upset with the shadow.

"I'm staying if you like it or not" Cole replied as he folded his arms, he rested his feet on the bed.

Talin didn't like the idea of sharing his private room with anyone, but when it came to shadows he knew that he couldn't trust any of them. His eyes narrowed dangerously, Talin was giving Cole the evil eye.

"Careful" the shadow remarked " or your face will stay that way". Talin turned his back on him, not thinking at all, he moved toward the door then out of the room. As he walked in a fast pace down the long corridore, Cole appeared at his side which startled him. "It's rude to leave a guest" Cole remarked, the elf turned on his heel sharply grabbing the shadow by the throat with his bare hands. He squessed but the shadow didn't feel a thing. "Get your hands off me this insteadly" the shadow commanded him.

"I will never listen to you, Cole" Talin said coldly now as he let go of him, he strolled away. "Don't follow me" Talin yelled at him as he entered a vast chamber that could over four thousand servants.

The walls weren't bare at all, all of them held weapons of all sorts. Some bigger than others, but all of them were just as deadly as the next. On the corners of each wall red drapes hang in place, giving the effect that this place were only for war.

Many centuries ago elves trained in this room to battle their enemies or wrong doer's but things have changed since then. Several drow warriors stopped what they were doing as Talin strolled up to them.

"Lord" all of them said at once then bowed to their leader.

"I want the ten of you to get Gemmel, alive would be nice. If any of you fail me, all of you will die" Talin commanded, they bowed once again.

"Right away,sir" they all said at once, then left the room in a hurry. Turning around, Talin felt he was being watched, his eyes shifted around the room. He hated the feeling since it felt like a ghost was in the room.

"Cole" he said coldly as two shadows appeared on both sides of him. He jumped, slightly frightened and embracanced. "Two" he said surprised to see two Shadows in the same room. "Who are you?" Talin demanded.

"Our names are not important" one of them said "Only Cole can control us".

Talin didn't like the sound of that at all, he leaned toward them. A scowl on his face, trying to make them frightened but it didn't work on them.

"What do you mean by us" Talin wondered as he asked the question, he said it in a calm way as he blinked. Cole entered the room a second later, he surveyed the room as he smiled, he was enjoying himself.

"I came here with a small army" Cole assured him.

The elf sneered not happy by the thought.

"What's your definison of a small army?" Talin growled, making him self very clear that he wasn't happy at all.

"About four thousand five hundred troops arrived with me" the shadow replied seeing Talin's reaction by the sheer noumber. His mouth hung open not being able to speak for a few minutes.

"four thousand, five hundred" Talin grasped in shook by the size of the small army.

Cole strolled over to the nearest wall and picked up a long sword, he held it out since he was studying it carefully.

"This looks new" he remarked coldly, Cole had seen it once before. A man used to carry it, a hero of the land that is now dead.

"It is, now replace it" Talin snarled with fury.

" Porter Lanster used to carry such a weapon, I thought he was unbeatible" Cole didn't replace the weapon just yet as he was getting off on upsetting Talin. He now at the elf seeing that anger that Talin had. "You should be more careful, your blood pressure would kill you one day" Cole informed him. He paused for a second "We want you alive, not dead" some of the shadows laughed at the joke.

Talin hated them for it, no one laughs at his expence and gets away with it. Cole could see that he had tread to far, he replaced the weapon and lifted his hand. A bottle of wine appeared from thin air, Cole handed it over to him as the elf smiled for once.

"I haven't had scream in years" Talin told him as he grabbed the bottle and left the room. Cole looked at his men with a nice smile.

"Keep an eye on him" Cole informed his troops then added " he will betray us".

The Land of Waller
Ten

A bad Idea

Standing posed, Gemmel moved to his right as a sword lashed at him. It came back, he dropped and rolled as he was trying to get out of the way. He lifted his own sword, as the other was blocked but the strike. His attacker backed up slightly, trying to see what to do next.

"You'll die" the orge snarled, then decided to jump into the air. Gemmel held out one hand, which froze the orge in midair, a puzzled expression filled it's face.

"NO" Gemmel said furous at the Orge. "You'll die by my hand" he strolled up to the frozen Orge and plunged his sword into the beast, it exploded once the heart was pearced, the body turned to ash within seconds. The group of orges and Orc's pulled back in fright.

"By Talin's order capture him" a new leader sprange up with the annoucement. The group eyed the crazy Orge as they moved aside.

"I would rather fight you" a Orc cried, then growled in warning. More than a hundred Orges moved away, spliting up in two groups as a single orge walked down the middle.

"Your insane, Quleck" an orge said then moved to the right side of the army that Gemmel faced.

"Talin must fail" an Orge said as an Orc snarled displeased by the annoucement. "Gemmel should die".

Gemmel watched in surprise as did the rest of the elves, they had no idea what was going on but at least they were learning about Talin’s plans for the boy. The leader snarled hatefully, wanting to get rid of the mutanteers.

“Then die” the new leader snarled, lifting it’s own weapon. The orc’s and orges charged into each other, hoping to cut down who ever questioned Talin’s orders.

Gemmel had backed up into the forest, where he and the elf’s watched from the forest, all of them were glad about the turnover for once. But now seeing a new threat was not a great thing, the elves weren’t ready to fight more enemies.

Two Orge’s died as a heavy axe split them apart, as several others either clubed each other or wound others. In the end only thirty of them were left, a single Orge bellowed at once.

The Tyranny of Talin

" We're free" only to see the sharp end of a sword, it looked down and saw to it's horror that it was stabed right through it's heart. A drow pulled his sword free, watching it's victim die.

"Kill the lot of them" that drow commanded as he looked at the forsest. "No one is free".

Gemmel and the rest of them were stunned by the sight of the drow. Bracer didn't dare smile as Gemmel had no idea who or what they were.

"Dear God" Bracer said only for effect.

"What is it?" Gemmel asked not sure what to feel nor do for that matter.

"We're dead, human. The drow are skilled warriors" Bracer informed his young friend. Linda only smirked at the thought, she knew what Bracer was up to.

"Not yet, we can get the others" Linda remarked

calmly as Bracer gazed over at her. Gemmel still had no idea what was going on, he was left out of the loop.

"Too much time" Bracer informed her, but she only smiled at the thought. "Into the wood" Bracer annouced to his tribe as they followed suite. Moving through the trees, the drow searched every where and yet they hadn't found a soul. They looked under every bush and rock that they came in contact with.

"Nothing over here" a single drow called out then another said the same thing, which somewhere off to his leaders right.

"That human has to be here somewhere" another drow said that had a bread.

D'mor hit him on the side of the head, he was

displeased with the out come, so far but he kept his men in line. At least they knew the truth.

"Gemmel isn't human, you twit" D'mor told them and sensed something nearby.

"What is he ? D'mor" one of his trusted allies asked.

"He's a powerful mage, that can destory us all. He betrayed Talen ten years ago, that's why he has no memory" D'mor stated as he looked up to see a branch move slightly in the wind. "Enough talk, where wasting time just standing here".

Taking two steps, four arrows hit the ground forcing him to stop moving.

"We have you surrounded drow" am angry elf said but D'mor wasn't convinced by the threat. Taking a single step, two of his men paid the prise of his foolish move.

"Give me the boy" D'mor demanded, playing his part in all of this. "And we'll leave" he assured them but he had enough of voiceless bodies. "Show your self" he said calmly.

More than two hundred elves appeared which made D'mor smile, he didn't flinch at all.

"So your banding together" D'mor spat.

Bracer stepped out from behind a tree and strolled up to him, he didn't dare smile but they needed information first.

"What news you bring us, D'mor" Bracer asked hoping that he would say something.

"Talin is getting stronger than you think, he needs this Gemmel to do something important" D'mor informed his old friend as a smile formed on his face for once.

The Tyranny of Talin

"You could help us, D'mor. Help us defect Talin, I know what you need to do to him. I know your pain, remember the day when he killed your parents." Bracer tried his best to convince his old friend, he noticed a single tear ran down the drows cheek. D'mor whispered softly into Bracers ear,

"I am helping" then pulled away and said in a loud voice for all to hear.

"He is our leader now, we'll die by his side" as another drow stepped up, hoping to get in on the conversation.

"Talin has done terrible things to all of us" this drow looked back at his comrades then turned back at the wood elves. His bald features, showed within the sun light. "As a nation, we will join your fight". D'mor shot him a look of approvel

The Land of Waller

Eleven

Danger Still lurks

Pushing open the door, Reid and his group watched it fall to the ground. Neither of them didn't know that it wasn't attached to the side. The four gazed into the rather large room. The walls, weren't covered with pictures at all, but at one point in history you could tell that they used to be. They were in awe since they were transfixed by the sheer beauty of the coloures. The floor had a redish pink carpet and in the middle of the room wasa great sword, which was housed in a glass pillor.

Light glistened off it, Rachel and the others moved into the room carefully, they separated and moved around, taking in what their eyes could see. None of them spoke since they were all breathless. But yet Rachel sensed that they were being watched, by what? They didn't know for certain. Yet it was there.

"The sword" Reid stated as he moved toward it, he took a single step, the display pillor started to enter the floor. Reid cried out he, turned to see he others. "I'm so sorry" he said guilt ridden.

His friends pointed up in horror, but Reid had no idea of what they were trying to do, but the way they pointed and the horror on their faces made him look over his shoulder.

He went white in horror as he looked at the beast, Reid had never seen nor lived through an attack by a giant bear. He looked at it's head, it had spikes. Reid now knew that this wasn't going to be easy at all, this was no bear. He looked at the feet, Reid was right the feet didn't match of a nornal bear, the feet were large like an elephant.

Bob started to shoot his bow and arrows, at last the arrows were magic so they could keep going.

Rachel used her magic, trying to stop the beast but it reared up on it's hind legs. It bellowed angrily, then slambed right down on the floor. All of them jumped just in time, since it was a shock wave.

Grabbing both his swords, Reid ran toward the beast. He struck at the first two legs, he ran around it getting out of the way.

The head of the beast lerched towards him, Reid stopped just a few inches away. He turned, as a set of fangs showed them selves as the gaint bear thing roared at him. Reid blew away the stink of the breath.

"You need a mint" Reid said joking around, but he was think of his next attack. An arrow hit it's left eye, it roared once again.

Reid saw his opening, he ran toward the hind legs, he jumped the hairs on the legs. Reid climbed for dear life, trying to hold on hoping that the beast would not know about him. Half way up it's leg, it shook itself.

Reid held on, Rachel attacked with a twister, trying to stop the thing from shaking. It succeeded, Reid climbed and climbed trying to find his way to the head. The bear thing, shook once again trying to dislodge the human but Reid held on as much as he could. Reaching the top of the bear thing at last, he could tell that the bear thing was about to get on it's hind legs once again.

Reid shouted out, as he started to slide but he grabbed onto the hairs. The shock wave came again, he looked down. He was glad to see that his two friends were not injured. Reid ran to the base of it's neck, he plunged the sword onto the neck causing it great pain.

The bear thing, went back up onto it's hind legs causing Reid to hang onto his sword. At least he was on the shoulders, but still he had to hang on until it came down again. Thinking fast, Reid grabed the fur on his left side. He pulled onto his sword, cutting into the skin, yanking it to the side. The bear thing roared one last time and fell dead as Reid held on.

Once back on the ground, Reid noticed the Rachel and Bob were sweating up a storm.

"You scared the two of us" Rachel said which was concerned for him "for a moment, I thought you were about to die".

"Come on let's grab this sword" Reid remarked trying to ignor the concern. Walking over, the pillor emgered. He punched the glass, but it didn't break at all. Reid held his hand, it hurt him.

Rachel giggled at the sight, but Reid wasn't in the mood at all.

"Boy's will be boy's" Rachel remarked only to herself but it caught Bob and Reid's attention. She smiled since she was toying with the two of them.

"Can you be any better Rachel" Reid interjected as she waved her hands over the glass, and then reached toward the glass. Something stopped her from reaching in, she didn't know what it was but she could feel it.

Reid and Bob laughed, seeing that Rachel had wasted her magic spell for nothing.Rachel looked around at first, tying to see what was holding her back.

"Reid move this level" Rachel said as he pulled the

level but nothing happened at all. Still she was puzzled, she looked at the other side of the pillor.

"Bob move the other level" he walked over a few steps and pulled on the level. It didn't move at all, both let of the levels.

"Seems we have a puzzle on oour hands" Reid mentioned, trying to thik how to open the case. Rachel walked around it, studying the device and the puzzle. She had noticed a punch pad and a single button of the other side.

"Lets try this again" Rachel said, both men stood on each side of the pillor. They awaited her commands, placeing her hand over the numbers on the pad. She launched a small magic spell, and pressed the button.

Both Reid and Bob pulled on the levels at the same time. The lid poped off the three of them, were happy to see that the lid had come off.

Reid reached for the hilt of the sword, but his hand touched glass which was now around the hilt of the sword.

"Not yet, there's glass around the hilt. We have to find out where the last part of this puzzle is" Reid said too busy to notice another beast.

Rachel and Bob looked at each other, both knew that they weren't going to get out of this just yet.

Reid noticed the stares over him, he moved his head. "Rachel find the last piece, Bob and I can handle it this time".

As the two battled the beast, Rachel looked around the room trying to find that last puzzle. She thought over the battle with the first bear giant, then the small puzzle that lay within the center of the room. The bear giant came close to her, but she avoided it as she launched a water spell at the creature. It yelped in pain, this bear giant was slower than the first. It rose into the air, since it was on it's hind legs. It smashed down, Rachel watched the pillor with renewed interest as the glass broke under the assult of the shock wave.

The sword fell to the floor at last, picking it up with her one hand she willed it to Reid. Sending it up to him, he grabbed onto it and plunged it into the beast killing it in one stroke.

Walking over to her, both men stared back at her in wonder, not sure how she got the sword out.

"How you…

"The bear giant smashed the glass with the shock wave. I was hovering at the time" Rachel informed the two. She now noticed some sort of sound, all three of them moaned not willing to kill another beast. The sound it self came off from their right, they wondered what was about to come in as they watched in amazement as a door swung open, spilling in light.

"What" Rachel grasped in surprise as Reid walked over to the door, his eyes were wide open as he looked at the gold. Reid couldn't believe his luck, he could pay off all his dedts and still live the life that he alone had dreamed about. But he knew he had a responcibility that he alone had to do.

Rachel and Bob followed suite, not believing their luck at all. All of them entered the vast chamber and pocket as much gold as they could carry.

Bob stashed some in his baclpack and into his pockets of his pants. The three left the room through another door and found them selves back in the main entrance.

Two elves stood in front of them and smiled warmly, neither cared what the three took.

"I see you survived, I take it you had a difficult time gettting the sword" one of the elves said as he smiled at them as the other grinned at them.

"I'm Tickerlance, call me Ticker for short, this here is Toperlous" the two elves introduced them selves as they bowed before the humans and the druid.

"Your not…

"We were sent to help you in your quest, I never thought you would make it out alive" Ticker interrupted Bob but he was plesent with all of them.

"Who sent you?" Reid questioned them hoping it would be good news. Both Elves grinned at each other as an another figure emerged from behind them. Reid now smiled, as he now saw an old friend of his.

"I should have known it was you, how are you Corp"Reid asked pleased to see him. Then thought of his immortal friend, he needed to get back to Tucker and free him. Something caught his eye, he looked over Corps shoulder, standing right behind him was the immortal not even frozen.

Twelve

When things go from Bad to worse

Sitting on Talin's bed Cole watched the water like substance in the bowl, trying to figure out what Talin was hidding from them. He knew something was wrong with the picture but didn't quite know what it was. The main door swung open revealing the dark master.

"Get away from my bed" Talin snarled with fury.

"What's eating yoy, Talin. Is it the new arrivels" Cole said to him coldly which Talin flinched at.

Talin never liked mountain Trolls since they were so unstable to control, but Sea Trolls were a lot more meaner and harder to to control. None trusted them, but Cole was the only one that could talk to them since regalur trolls were now fighting each other.

Getting up from the bed, Cole strooled over to Talin who by the way looked as if his head was about to pop off. Cole only sneared at him, trying to get a reaction out of him.

"This isn't your chambers anymore, as of right now you are no longer in command of this war". Cole muttered a magic spell under his breath, which striped Talin of his powers. He shivered as if he were cold, his head bent down.

"Where am I?" the elf said now afriad for the first time in his life.

"Don't you remember" cole stated a bit surprised at the comment.

"The last thing I remember is I was traveling with friends to battle Morsurrel" Talin said as he now looked at his hands, he now knew that it was sixteen years ago. He looked up at Cole, terror filled his soul as he realized now that he was in the precence of evil..

Cole just stood there pleased to be rid of the evil Talin once and for all. Placing his hands on either side of Talin's heaad, the elf looked as if were about to faint.

"What are you doing?" Talin asked in wonder as he now felt lite headed. He yawned as he slumbed to the ground, he was now asleep. As Cole waved his hands over the body, it disappeared a moment later.

"Now Talin, after you learn your lesson then we shall see who will be master" Cole laughed mocking the idea that Talin would be able to survive on his own.

*　　　*　　　*

D'mor studied the group of elves carefully, he

didn't wish to upset them but at the same time he knew that this was going to hard for all of them.

"So where is this boy? That calls himself Gemmel" D'mor wondered not really interested in any treaty.

"I'm not a boy" Gemmel announced as he stepped into the small clearing. All eyes went to him, the drow looked stunned by his appearance.

"Talin has corrrupted you as he did with me. But it's Cole that you should be aware of" D'mor replied as he studied the young man that looked far to young to be slightly over forty five years. The drow had heard of the mighty shadow, that used to be part of his own race. His face was as cold as of his own manners "Though you should never speak his name to me since it only means death and betrayel. He has disowned his kind".

Gemmel and the elves were surprised by the news,

they had no idea that Cole was a threat to them. Though some of them knew that the shadow was up to something even worse than they had ever imagined. Moving slightly, something up in the sky caught Gemmel's attention. He smiled sligtly, seeing his friend at long last.

"Corp" Gemmel said which caught the drows attention as much as the elves. As he gazed up at the roc/ elf Gemmel now noticed that there was figures on his back. The drow shield their eye's as the half breed flew toward them.

Landing a minute later, the four figures climbed off the roc. Gemmel gazed at the immortal, as Corp changed shape. All of them walked toward the group, Gemmel had seen them once before.

"You must be Gemmel" Reid said as he bowed

before the boy, who was taking aback.

"Why do you bow before me? I'm not a king nor someone important" Gemmel wondered, since he was slightly puzzled by the reaction.

"Don't you remember" Bracer said as he explaned "His father once surved under your command". He turned slightly to Reid but not by much. "Reid here is king of this country,you're his cousin". Bracer informed the group as Linda walked up to them.

Gemmel watched her with interest as she strolled past him, he and everyone else saw the two kiss.

"So this is your husband" Gemmel said feeling foolish by his attempt. But yet, he knew that he needed to get past his own feelings. Images flew around in his head, as his memory regaining it self.

Shakinghis head Gemmel now remembered his own past, and how he fell into darkness. It was true,

Reid's father did serve under him at one point since he was a warlord at one point in life.

"Yes, I now remember. It's good to see you cousin, where are the other two elves that we sent to help you in your quest". Gemmel asked in concern.

"Petals attacked us while we were trying to escape. The two of them gave their lives to help us escape" Reid stated, trying to understand how the boy knew about the elves.

Reid just stood there waiting for a reply as the others stared at the boy, the drow were speachless not only knowing what was going on but how did Gemmel knew anything about the two elves.

"I over heard Bracer, I didn't mean to it's just I was in the area and I … Gemmel looked embarenced by the thought. But at last he was amitting it to them.

Gemmel faced toward the drow commander, D'mor wanted to know who was in command so he could take orders.

" I take it you want to know who you serve now, well I can tell you that you no longer serve darkness, Talin or Cole any more. You now serve me" Gemmel informed the drow who looked releaved.

"What are you doing?" Corp asked not liking the sound of what Gemmel was saying, nor implying.

"I'm returning to Talin and Cole. These drow are mine now, we will act as spies for you since we need to know what is going on" Gemmel reassured them all. Every one smiled at the thought, this fight was about to begin.

* * *

Opening his eye's for the first time, Talin shook

his head to get the last of the sleep out of his eyes.

Looking around at last, he noticed that he wasn't alone at all since he noticed a man walk up to him.

Turning his head slightly, Talin noticed the out line of a forest.

"Where am I?" Talin wondered, he snapped his fingers. Testing if he still had magic, the brush near him burst into flame.

"Your near White Grove" a voice said from behind him, once back on his feet. Talin smiled at last, he knew Cole would do this to him so he prepared for it.

"White Grove" Talin scoffed now facing the man that stood before him as he studied his clothes. He now knew that he wasn't in his home country.

'Your not from around here are you?' the beared man said as he picked at his teeth.

"No , I'm not. I'm from Waller" Talin informed the strangeer, as he snickered testing his magic even more.

"Waller" Gary said, impressed by the man, He knew that it was a long walk to it and it was a feat to do it. "That's a long way from here. Well, welcome to Deny" the stranger welcomed the guest.

Talin had heard of the far off land, he had never imagine that he was two thousand miles away from Waller, but here he was. He smiled wickedly, testing the man further.

"Who rules this land?" the elf asked.

"I do" Gary teased, he felt a blade enter his heart. Talin pulled it out as he watched the man die as blood sputtered out of his mouth, the body twiched for a second then was still.

Cole thought he could take the madness away from

the elf but he never thought that Talin may have covered his own. But this wasn't so since Talin had fooled the shadow and with his own acting.

"Now I rule Deny" Talin cheered, as he felt Gary's own magic enter him. Once the transfer was down he bent down and cut the head off the body.

"What are you doing there? And why did you take that mans head off his body?" a troll said as it strolled up to the elf. It wanted to kill the stranger for this very act.

The troll stopped moving, it struggled but couldn't get free. It roar a warning, not pleased by the trap.

"Tell me" Talin said evilly. "Who is your master?" but the Troll gazed at him.

"You killed him, M'lin will kill you for your disobendence elf" the troll answered.

The Tyranny of Talin

" I thought he was your master" Talin pointed to the dead body.

"That is M'lin's brother. M'lin is my true master, my savior and my hope to bring terror to this land. He will hurt you elf" the troll answered sadened by his loss. Talin blinked taking control of the beast, He needed to get to this so called M'lin and do him in.

"Now you serve a greater evil, fear my name. Fear my temper, for I am Talin the Mighty". Talin informed the troll. It looked shocked at the name, he knew of him and his repartation. The troll bowed his head to his new master. "M'lin will fall" Talin reassured him as he now was seeing his opportunity for a greater role than he had ever faced before. The beast stood tall waiting for his instructions. "Gather your kind and any who would follow me" Talin stated, feeling his own pride swell up.

*   *   *

Cole opened his mouth then decided to shut it not knowing what to say or do in any matter. His forces gathered behind him, a whole army of monsters that would do hi bidding and his own kind that would back him up in an instant. He turned to face his army that filled the vast chamber and yet it went beyond it's very walls. His voice rang out, it was devilish, greedy and nasty all at once.

"WAllER IS OURS" he cried out as his eyes turned red with pure hatred.

Thirteen

Ungodly

Bob shoved his friend away trying to get some distance from him and he didn't know what to say since he was upset.

"How dare you" Bob accussed his friend.

"Gemmel gave me no choice in the matter" Reid pleaded trying to calm his old friend.

"I won't give it up, not to him nor to you" Bob stated heatedly purely upset that Gemmel wanted the gold.

"Just give him the gold" Reid now yelled back.

"We found it, we keep it" Bob yelled back not pleased with the outcome

"GIVE IT NOW" Reid started to shout since his

friend wasn't willing to listen to reason.

"Bugger off" Bob now snarled as Reid grabbed him by the collar, both struggled but Bobs pants tore in the attempt as gold coins fell to the ground.

Moving away Bob winked at Reid before turning his back on him. This was only for show since Gemmel was watching them, neither wanted to give up the gold at all. At least the two had put up a show since the others were watching them, gold coins laid on the ground. All of them fake, but to look at anyone would think they were real.

Rachel bowed her head as she entered a tent just a few feet away.

"Rachel" an image of a flooting head said as she looked in the direction of the voice.

"Garnel, is something wrong?" Rachel dared to ask

trying to forget about the excahnge between Bob and Reid.

"The druid counsel has summoned you" Garnel Gel remarked as the image disappeared a second later. Rachel couldn't fathom why the counsel had summoned her at this hour at all, they knew that it was critical to keep the members together. Yet she knew that she had to go, the gang was becoming separated from each other and Rachel didn't like it at all. Looking through a crack , she somehow knew that Bob and Reid was up to something. All of them lied about the two elves that helped them, but for some reason Reid was playing it safe.

Turning around, Reid made it look like he was still angry at Bob. As he stared at Rachel's tent, seeing that she had left.

"I wish you well, Rachel" Reid muttered as he

glanced over his shoulder to see Bob, but he knew he wasn't there at all.

Separated at last, Reid thought. Bob will find out what happened to Gemmel and why Talin's army had grown stronger. His mind was on other things as well, he missed his wife and Reid knew that it would to soon to see Linda again.

Walking over to the great half breed, Corp changed into the roc and cocked his head to the side to watch his friend.

"I take it Gemmel took the ruse" Corp asked.

"He did and everyone else" Reid informed him, as they took flight a minute later.

* * *

Strolling into a vast hall, drapes hung down on either side of the lone figure. Rachel studied each member of the councel as she approched them, everyone of them were human, all but one. This room had no use for a table, but it had more than plenty of chairs.

"You sommoned me" Rachel broke the silence as one of them members stood at last. She looked at the bald man, that stood at six feet tall.

"We did, this is about Talin" Gary said as he stood infront of his chair not willing to move toward her.

"What about him" Rachel wondered.

"He's up to no good, Cole sent him to Deny but he tricked Cole into thinking that his powers were gone. He's taken control of the small country" Gary informed her. All of them knew something about this before hand, it was their spy that had told them of the exchange.

"So the Tyranny of Tyranny of Talin has begun" Rachel stated not surprised in the least.

"As Weten predicted" another of the councel said, which now stood on Gary's left side.

"What do you want me to do about it?" Rachel wondered playfully knowing all to well what they would say.

"Give him the power to rule this country" the entire counsel said all at once as each and every eye turned red with pure hatred.

* * *

Standing in front of the anceint building, Bob had returned to the deadly forest to help the two elves, he smiled at them since he was also hidding a secret.

"What did you find out?" Bob asked the two, who had done some spying for him.

"Cole has kicked Talin out of the country and is gaining strengh as we speak" Ticker said, then looked over his shoulder. Fearful that someone may be over hearing this converation.

"Gemmel did speak the truth, but I fear he might have taken on too much for his own good" Toperlous stated as he itched his head. "He's acting evil, to trick Cole and Talin but he is using way to much magic".

"Reid doesn't know what I am, never has" Bob stated "None have witnessed my power in centuries, I alone will stop them"

Both elves bowed their head toward him, his form changed a little. A bright light surrounded Bob his face stayed the same except his clothes.

"All hail, Slem the mighty" both elves chanted as they watched him change into the god that they loved.

"Gather everyone" Bob told the two. "We have a war to win" as he spread his arms, his magic woke the surrounding forest, beasts that killed turned back into the pieceful beings that they were. Trees up rooted them selves, elves, gnomes and forgotten creatures came alive once more. This army was big, it was bigger than any could fathom, it was huge.

"You want a war Cole, you just got your wish" Bob stated with an evil smile. "Your arse is mine".

Fourteen

A fearful thing

Strolling into his chamber, Cole smiled at seeing Gemmel which stood infront of him. He knew that Gemmel had betrayed the others, but for some reason, both of them were playing some sort of game with Talin.

"So the forgotten boy returns to claim his throne once again", Cole said with distaste.

"No" Gemmel said as he pointed over to the bed "But he has" as Cole looked over at the bed shocked to see Talin, he staggered back a few feet.

"I thought you were powerless" Cole said out oud, trying to fathom why Talin had returned in the first place.

"Guess again Cole, this time it'll be you that shall die" as Talin stood up and then approched the shadow with mock hatred. Gemmel stood in the middle, holding each other back. Both wanted to tear each other apart.

"Stop this now" Gemmel shouted which caught their attention. "If we're going to rid of goodness, we have to unite with each other not squarble with each other".

Talin gazed at him in surprise as Cole backed up a few steps, they never knew that Gemmel had a back bone, but his logic sounded right to them.

"Your right, Gemmel." Cole said voicing both their thoughts. Talin smiled evilly at the shadow, showing his displeaser.

"I've taken control of Deny" Talin annouced as

Cole laughed at the mere thought of it.

"That small country, that's miles away from here" Cole pointed out, not realizing that this was not an image of Talin.

"Not anymore" Talin snapped a little to sharply "This isn't an image of me fool, I'm here in flesh and blood. My army is here, ready to go to war once more, my strengh is growing beyond Deny now, it's now in Oper. Slowly making it's way here, my army grows every day as they draw even closer".

Cole stepped toward him shocked by the truth of the matter, he touched Talin with one of his fingers. He smiled wickedly at the idea.

"Should I" he wondered out loud. "Yes, I really should" Cole rejoiced at the thought as he summoned four of his greatest shadows, beings of supream terror.

The bedroom door opened as four shadow warriors entered the room. Each studying the wall, the floor and the bed. They stood proud before the three, Talin waved his left hand as a hidden door appeared just behind him.

"Once your on the other side go into each each country and spread our terror. Build our army, and come back the long way" Cole instructed his men.

The four didn't hesitate nor questioned him at all, they walked over to the portal. Each spoke in a whisper of what country they would rule over, one by one they disappeared.

The three laughed enjoying a joke of some sort, but for Gemmel he had made sure that he was covering his tracks.

*   *   *

Sitting what seemed like a life time Reid finally got up. He was alone for now, he knew that Corp would be back soon.

"What have we done wrong?" Reid wondered, as he shook his head.

"Nothing" a voice said from behind him, Reid turned to see Corp transform. He smiled weakly since it was good to see his old friend once again.

"We've done nothing wrong, the elves didn't push him hard enough".

"How can you be so calm about all this? Gemmel has reunited with Cole and who knows what is behind all of this" Reid said, he didn't know that Gemmel was really spying or not but what ever it was they needed to know.

"Time will tell and we must believe that hope will

survive". Corp stated trying not to tell too much to his human friend since he knew more than he was letting on. Reid shook his heead trying to understand what the half breed was trying to say to him. "We better go" he suggested to Reid "You got to pay off your debts and make new friends. This war won't win on it's own".

Both walked toward the village where Reid had grown up.

"Look at that" Reid said with a smile. "I hadn't seen that flag in over a decade".

Corp studied the flag with interestm two swords criss crossed over each other with black in the back ground. "Welcome Corp" Reid said happy to be home at last "To Two Swords, were the beggers are hanged and the rich stay rich".

A second later both entered the village and a scream could be heard. There were people everywhere, a markey was on as a band in the center of the village played for them. It was hard to hear since they were loud, you had to yell at each other to be heard, Reid smiled once more enjoying the music. "NOW THIS IS HOME" he shouted to his friend.

Corp nodded in agreement, but the music was too loud for him.

"lively" he stated as a few girls walked by looking his way and giggled which he couldn't hear. Reid couldn't hear what his friend was saying but he dismissed it for now.

"HASN'T CHANGED A BIT,CORP. THAT'S WHERE I USED TO HANG OUT" Reid informed him as he pointed to the pub. He turned slightly to see an old friend of his. The round man patted his stomach as he swallowed the last of his drink then belched loudly.

"GOOD TO SEE YOU MATE" Bill said drunkenly then farted.

"I SEE YOU'VE IMPROVED, BILL. FIRST IT WAS THE BELCH, THAT REAKED BY THE WAY, BUT THE FART THAT SURE WILL KEEP THE LADIES AWAY". Reid stated as he waved the air with his hand.

Bill moved away as he guided the two to the pub to get a fresh drink, a couple of women didn't see where they were going, Bill farted once more.

"BILL THAT'S GASTLY" a red head said which stood at least five eight as the other stood at least an inch shorter. Both held their nose, trying to block the stink as they walked away.

The three entered the pub as Bill bellowed out

"The boy's home old mom and he brought a friend with him". Everyone stopped talking and turned their heads a few murmured ashtinished that Reid had returned. The band stopped for a single moment, as a cheer went up glade to see their old comrade in arms.

A striking attractive older woman walked out of the kitchen, her brownish hair swung at her shoulders.

"Come on" Lynn said not knowning why no one was talking. "What's with all this silence" the older woman gaze fell onto the hansom man, she smiled for the first time. "Reid it's good to see you again" as he strolled up to her. Both of them huged, both of them were so happy to see each other. Reid was overjoyed to see her at last.

"Hi mom" Reid said then embraced her once more.

"You've gained some weight" Lynn told him as she patted his stomach. He turned back to see Corp only to see every beer mug raised in the air.

"A toast to Reid" Bill stated as he munched on a piece of toast "A heroes return".

Corp laughed at the thought which caught eveyones attention. He stopped, after a few minutes.

"What are you laughing at?" Lynn asked not sure who or what the elf was in any matter.

" He's not a hero, a very rich king yes, but he surely isn't a hero" Corp stated but was intreged with Lynn.

"My son isn't a king, by birth yes and he isn't rich at all" Lynn exclaimed as Reid lifted two bags of gold from his pack back that he had set down after he huged his mother.

" I struck it rich. After I slayed two mighty giants. I have enough to not only pay off my debts but I could buy this village ten times over and still have more than enough gold. After I buy everyone of you a drink". Reid stated then added "if that toast you gave for me is still in your mouth. You can keep it".

Bill chocked on the toast as he tried not to laugh, a few people found it funny since they were all ready drunk. Not only the pub, but the entire village cheered for his success and for that extra beer. Standing around a table a minute later, Corp studied his friend not sure what to make of the speech at all.

"Why don't you tell your mother of what you've become" Corp pointed out as Reid eyed him

questionly.

"It'll break her heart, Corp" Reid replied of which she over heard.

"Reid, dear I all ready know" Lynn remarked calmly "I do hear things about you and what you've done over the years".

"What do you know? Answer me that and I 'll drop it" Reid replied trying to hold back his emotons just in case. He prided him self over the ability that he can overcome his emotions but not all the time.

" I might be old, but I know what you've become young man. You're a bounty hunter for hire" she let it sink in for a second as he gazed at her. "I don't care less if your King of this country or not at least I'm happy that your happy at what you do" Lynn stated as he looked amazed that she actually knew of his position.

"Anyway, that man over there wants his money back" she pointed to the assassin who sat at a table it looked as if he were alone. Reid glanced over at the table only seeing him, a slight smile formed on his face.

"Jhet" Reid said amazed to see the assassin at all, he had never figured of seeing him ever again. But there he was, sitting at a table as someone tried to joke with him. "I better pay him double for the long wait".

He surmissed, feeling guilty for not doing the job at all.Walking over to the table, he laid down ten gold coins since Reid was only looking at him.

"What's this for?" Jhet remarked not really knowing why there was money on the table in the first place.

"I didn't get Gemmel for you, so as a token I'm

paying you back with ten gold coins" Reid informed the assassin hoping not to start a fight of some sort. Jhet pointed across the table to the young man who sat across from him.

"Tucker your free to go" Jhet said calmly, since he didn't want any trouble at all. It wasn't his nature to to stand out of the crowd, he preferred to stay hidden from sight.

Reid turned his head sharply startled to hear and see his immortal friend, he had forgotten all about the immortal since they had to leave that horrible forest. A smile spread across his face, as he watched his old friend.

"Did he harm you in anyway?" Reid sounded concern for the immortals well beinging.

"No, he didn't harm me at all. Jhet was concerned

that you forgot about me. After you rushed away on Corp, I simply made my way back to the field trying to avoid so many creatures. After I cleared the forest, I met up with Jhet here. He saved me from a beast, of which I'm greatful by the way" Tucker remarked as he informed his friend of the fight.

"Remarkable" Reid said, glad that his friend was unhurt from his encounter from the To'wish. A legendary creature that could rip a human to pieces, but it didn't stop the assassin from doing his job.

"Anyway we walked to the nearest village and slowly made our way here. I knew that we would meet again, Jhet here has more talents than you have" Tucker remarked with pride which put the assassin on the spot. The village shook, but no ne payed any attention to it except Corp.

"What's going on?" Corp grasped not really

speaking to anyone at all.

"Come over here?" Tucker shouted over the music and waved the half breed over to the table. A waitress placed four beers down on the table as Corp eyed the beer with interest.

"I better not" Corp warned them, he knew what would happen if he were to drink it.

"Go on" Jhet pushed him "it won't hurt you". The half breed lifted the mug and took a sip of it, it had been a long time since he had a good drink of beer.

"Tastes good" Corp said at last as a great loud fart escaped from him which was louder than anyone had ever heard before. Every head in the pub glanced toward them.

"Now that's a fart" an old man said then smiffed

the air as did everyone else, they all held their nose's.

"That's some fart" a waitress said as she waved with her other hand infront of her as she held her nose with the other. Two men entered the main door, both of them gaged at the stink.

"Lynn" one of the men said "Did Bill bring down the house?" which everyone laughed at the joke. "Or did his mother walk through the back door" since she smelled worse than him which caused everyone to keep laughing.

Once the laughter died off, the door and the windows were opened since it smelled really bad in the place. Lynn pushed the beer over to her son who took it gladly.

"You better stick to water" Lynn suggested to Corp which blushed at the thought as she smiled at him.

"I better for the rest of the night" he replied in

agreement.

"I've set up your rooms for the next few nights which I hope you'll like" she mentioned to them and smiled playfully at Corp. Reid smiled openly seeing his friend blush once more as Lynn made her exit.

"Mom really fancies you" Reid informed his friend.

"I can see that, but no. She's not my type, besides it's against the rules" as he got to his feet and yawned from the long journey. "I bid you a good night" Corp said as he moved off as a waitress pointed to his room.

"I'll meet you soon, darling" Susan said which caught Reid off guard.

"Against the rules indeed, I wonder…" Reid said to himself as he thought a moment of why he had said thet. "I guess mother's a bit to sharp for him or he's the one that likes to make the first move".

As the sun crested the morning sky the following day, Reid and his friends walked around the market. None of them paid to much attention to the crowd, children ran around them excitedly enjoying the morning air.

"Harry, come here" a woman shouted over the sound of the soft music as he scampered off towards his friends. Only to be blocked by a five foot nine muscle man, that had a sword straped to his back for safe keeping. His tattoo of a red dragon was on his chest, as Harry stared at it for a moment.

"Outter my way" Harry said rudely which the bald man did not like, he looked down at the boy . A pleasant smile was on his face, as he studied the boy. His other tattoo of another dragon was on his right upper arm, it moved slightly as the man flexed his muscles.

"I will not move until you say please" the muscle man said trying to be nice to the boy.

"Please won't get you anything" Harry snapped at him, trying to go around him but the muscle man would not let him go.

Both Reid and Corp saw the exchange, but Reid was more interested in what would happen next. He noticed his sister walked up sternly over to her nephew, a smile formed on Reid's face as he watched patiently.

"None of that now!" an old man said to Harry but the boy refused to listen to any of them. He takes after me, Reid thought.

"Respect your elders, young man" the grey haird old man said as he pointed out.

"Respect this" Harry said sharply annoyed at the two then gave them a rude sign with his fingers.

"Harry" his Aunt said agast at what he did.

"Aunt" Harry began only to be interrupted.

"Don't Aunt me, young man. For that, you can't play with your friends at all" Alice said as she grabbed onto his collar. "What do you say to these nice men" Alice remarked trying to remain calm through out the exchange. She remember a time when Reid behaved like this with their own mother.

"Sorry sirs" the boy said without meanin it but it sounded sincer. Turning around Alice smiled openly as she let the boy go as she hugged her brother.

"Reid, I heard you were back and with a friend no doubt" Alice remarked as she noticed Tucker and Corp walk up to them. "Tucker it's good to see you again".

"It's good to see you too Alice" Tucker replied as he shook her hand.

"I'm Corp" Corp introduced himself as he extended his hand. She gazed at him since Alice had never any elf before.

"Nice to meet an elf at long last" Alice said, taking in the beauty of the figure. The morning sun hightened his skin, her mouth hung open as she had a sparkle in her eyes.

"I'm not an elf, a half breed" Corp informed her, as she studied him up and down growing ever more excited by the second.

"Half elf and what?" Alice asked intreged at the thought.

"I'm also a Roc" Corp finally answered her

question. Alice beamed with pleaser, Reid noticed the way his sister was looking at Corp.

"A morph, I heard such stories about your kind. That you could change into a great beautiful bird and walk just like us. I never imagined that Reid would have a handsome friend, such as you" Alice stated with amazement at meeting such a creature. She looked at him warmly then decided to look at her brother. "I better go find your son" she said to Reid as she gave him a kiss on the cheek then ran off.

"I didn't know you were married!" Corp said regreted by the thought but was happy for Reid.

"I haven't had time to mention it besides Alice is my sister, not my wife" Reid stated but he knew half of it was a lie. He glanced up to see a man standing on the raised platform.

"Come now and come forth, gather around me as tall as you are, like mountains before me" the man said as the ground began to shake and only Corp noticed it. "Come upon the sky, to join the moon and the sun since we gather for you".

Corp slowly walked over to the edge of the village to see what was happening. Nothing but dust blinded him.

"Now our secret is revealed , this is not a village nor a town you stand in but of a great and powerful city". But still the man didn't stop to hesitate, "Now it's our turn, for beware Talin and Cole. We are a force worth reakoning".

Corp turned around in surprise by the statement as shock sunk in by the words, he turned back once more. He ran toward the edge of the city, feeling the ground rise in the air. Two men ruched toward him from making a grave mistake as Corp dove into the sky below . He changed form Quickly as he took flight. The two men, sighed with releaf now knowing what he was.

The wind caught him in his decent and made him rise with the current of the air, Corp looked all about noticing for the first time that Two Swords was the center pillar as four other villages could be seen. He flew pass one of the villages, taking in the breath taking beauty of the ancent hiddin city.

The five villiages were at the top, Corp flew past windows on the side of it. People stared at him, several waved openly greating him to their grand city.

Corp heard all of them sing their mighty song,

which up lifted his spirits. He took in the view of the tree line and the bushes, all of it were unharmed by the shacking of the ground. Turning back to his starting point he saw Reid wave his arms in the air to get his attention. Many on lookers gazed in amazement at him, all of them welcomed him.

Landing on his feet, he changed back to the elf as a young boy stood infront of him amazed to see something different. No one moved nor said anything at first since they were shocked by the transfermantion.

"You're a morph" Harry said as he couldn't take his eyes of him.

"That I am since your father and I are friends" Corp sprouted cheerfullt. Reid moved through the crowd of people, Harry turned about and noticed him. A smile formed on his face, he was very happy to see him.

"D-Dad" Harry said excitedly and rushed over to him with his arms open, they both hugged as if they were one.

The crowd parted for the first time revealing his Aunt. Alice looked crossed and annoyed but now noticed that he was with his father. Her mood shifted and a warm and friendly smile was on her face.

"I told you that your dad would come back" Alice said smuggly. Corp just stood there unsure of what had happened, not for Reid's family but for the villages.

"What's going on?" Corp demanded still puzzled by the ancent city. "Is this a village or not". Both Reid and Alice looked at him, but another speaker caught their attention.

"We've kept this a secret for countless years, Morph. Two Sword's isn't a village nor a town, it's an enormous city" the bald man retorted, which stood at least six feet tall.

Corp smiled bouldly since the news and the shock was finally sinking into him for once.

"Cole" he said coldly. "We just grew stronger than you think".

Fifteen

A Nasty thing happens

Walking through a veil of white light, Rachel saw the on lookers which are Bob's army and followers. Her eyes shifted to the center of the camp as she smiled warmly to the anicent god.

" I see you turned back to your true self, O' mighty lord" Rachel said, pleased for him and for their cause since they needed all the help they could get.

"I told you once and I'l tell you again just call me Bob" Bob replied a little to harshly then added changed his manners all together. He now smiled warmly trying to forget about his harsh tone. "Has Reid done his task"

"He did so and more, Reid found Tucker and Jhet in Two Swords, but for some reason he's holding back on something. As if he's trying to hide of who he is" Rachel said which she could not place.

The two now stood silent for a few seconds, Bob's followers were getting ready for battle. Some laughed at jokes while others practiced with their swords. All but one just didn't do anything at all.

"Practice fool were about to go to war" a great Centaur exclaimed as it stood over the female, trying to threaten her.

"I wasn't summoned like you, I was here before you came" Linda pointed out, trying to stay calm the whole time. His eyes narrowed not trusting her at all but for some reason, he couldn't keep away from her since she was drawing him in.

"Who are you lady? And why are you so confident?" another centaur asked as an arrow was shot his way, he caught it with his left hand as he grinned.

"I'm Linda and I'm Reid's wife" she commented seeing the others surround her, they all murmured surprised to be in the precence of Reid's wife.

"You're the famous Linda" a bearded gnome remarked and brightened with glee. "I'm humble to be in the precence of a mighty elf qeen like you. My name is Promose" he introduced himself at last.

"I'm no qeen" Linda remarked but it was nice of him to think so. "Those two are my friends, Bob and Rachel. I help them from time to time" she stated matter of flatly.

The three believed her of caurse as she left them since she was strolling over to her friends.

"Rachel" Linda said with arms wide the two hugged openly.

"Linda, how are you girl?" Rachel wondered glade to see her friend smile.

"Get back here" a large man shouted to a halfling which interrupted the confersation. "I'm going to kill you, you little runt" he threatened angirly.

Racing over to the two of them Rachel got in the middle of them, two elves held the halfling back as two others tried to stop the large man.

"If you kill him Gailth, I 'll be forced to tell your dad" Rachel said sternly as she shook with rage. The halfing didn't say a thing, instead he handed the jewel back. "What's this?" Rachel grasped with puzzlement.

"I took this from him, I don't want to die by a

Narc, so here" the halfling said defeatedly since he was going to sell it anyway.

The large man tock it from him as he eye the jewel making sure it wasn't a fake.

"Try that again and I'll stick ye" the narc said not trusting the halfling at all. The halfling scurried away, no longer wanting to be around the narc at all. Rachel seemed pleased by the out come, but she knew the ohters were on edge as well.

A noise could be heard from behind her, Rachel turned her head to see what it was as a drow dropped to the ground harder than it would have liked.

"Well, look we have here" a gaint stated as he stepped up and lifted the drow with one hand.

"Let go of me" the drow hissed angrily trying to swing his baldes at the wrist but the gaint paid no hed since it didn't feel pain.

"Why are you here drow?" Rachel grasped in horror "to spy on us, perhaps". The dark skinned elf put his weapons away, making sure that he didn't threatened anyone at all.

"I see I'm out matched" he admitted feeling a fool for coming here in the first place, he bit down on his teeth trying to make one of his teeth to seep poison into himself. "You won't get anything out of me since I'm all ready dead".

A hand shot out from the bushes which everyone could see, Rachel just smiled at the drow who was still standing.

"What ever you learned from us now stays with us" she remarked to the drow, he loathed the truth since he had plainly forgotten to contact Cole. He waited for the poison to take effect, but for some reason it wasn't working. Four big gaints lumbed up from behind the drow, as Rachel now smiled pleased to have a drow prisoner. "I turned your poison to water, by the way" she informed the drow prisoner.

The drow stared at her as he was being lead away, as he scawled at her. He knew that he was peged, and he didn't like the feeling.

*　　　　*　　　　*

Over looking his men as they left the base, cole stood with a cold look on his face. He didn't grin nor smiled since it was beyond his nature. Shadows never really did smile but if they did it was only inspite for their comrades or enemies. Talin stood on one side and Gemmel the other, none of them spoke nor thought a thing.

The rush they all felt was within their bones since they knew that they would win, but cole moved slightly as he decided to leave the two.

Walking into a vast chamber, were everyone worked out, Cole knew that he wasn't alone at all.

"Who's there" cole demanded unpleasantly as two tall ugly creatures appeared in front of him. Neither of them could be discribed since they were too terrifying to distribe in the first place. Their faces were hidden in darkness, they didn't floot like ghosts nor spirits. These were worse, they are known as the scribe, they eat souls.

"One of your followers is a spy" Haimis informed the shadow master.

"I know Talin needs to go" Cole annouced as he grinned wickedly. "That's one of the reasons I sent his troops instead of mine".

"Now that's been done, what about Gemmel?" the

other asked.

"Gemmel , what about him?" Cole narrowed his eye lid's not liking the way the conversation was going. Cole flexed his muscles, as his face lumbed near one of them.

"He's making waves" Haimis insistant then glanced quickly to his counterpart. "He has…

"Enough" Cole thundered with anger "I trust him with my life, he will kill Talin no matter what, but if your insisting that he's a traitor. I'll rip your heads off and have them hang on my walls" he seathed with anger, trying despretly to calm down as the two looked frightened at the thought. Neither of them wanted to be killed, as if it were possible anyway.

"So sorry, we didn't want to imply such a thing, we were more concerned with him" Haimis replied while shaking since he couldn't stop from being frightened , the two disappeared a second later.

"I surrounded by fools" Cole remarked as he turned toward the doors only to see Talin pushing open the doors.

"You want me dead" the elf snapped bitterly.

"I…"

"Don't I me, Cole. I've known from the start that you favour Gemmel than me. Really I don't blame you…" Talin was mad like hell but his movement was frozen .Cole noticed that Talin was frozen on the spot then decided to look over his shoulder and noticed a white light as a figure emerged from it.

"Looks like I got here in time" a female voice said as Cole glanced over to her trying not to smile at all.

"That you did, please erace his current memory. He just learned that he's about to die" Cole remarked matter of flatterly. Rachel winked at Cole as she smiled at him since she strolled over to Talin.

Blowing him a kiss, she watched the frozen elf for a single moment.

"He'll not only forget but I also granted him a wish" Rachel informed the shadow.

"What was his wish?" Cole dared to ask, wondering what the druid had done to the elf.

"He's more powerful than you I'm afraid, but do not fear it won't last beyond this day" Racel played with them both and walked away. Cole finally smiled, what looked more like a scowl as she disappeared.

"For hating me" Talin said once he was unfrozen, as he wondered why he had said that. He looked puzzled for a moment or two. "Did you summon me?" he asked the shadow.

Cole remarked and thought fast, trying to cover his tracks.

"Yes I did now take your men to Two Swords and dispose of the village" Cole ordered him. The elf turned around and left the shadow to ponder what to do, he grinned to himself. "May the game begin".

Sixteen

A scheme of play

Rumiging through his belongings Tucker glanced over his shoulder to look in the other storage bin.

"Where are my…" he found what he was looking for. "Yes" he snapped happily as he drew out his two long blades. Reid sat in a cahir seeing the blades which made him smile, he knew that his friend was now ready.

"Where's Corp?" the immortal asked.

"He's flying about I guess. Corp has been gone for a while" Reid admitted as he thought about it.

"He might be getting more troops for this insane war we're about to have" Tucker remarked, hating the idea of hurting any creature.

"I dought that, we have more than enough troops and to keep that giant lizard at bay" Reid remarked as he then looked up at the sky to see a great bird coming toward them. Landing a moment later, Corp looked a little fraziled.

"Corp are you all right?" Reid and Tucker asked at the same time, unsure what he might say.

"Talin's army is on its way, which is the good news. The bad news is they destroyed hemel on the way" Corp annoucened to the surrounding crowd. A man smasked the palm of his hand.

"I had a sister there" he said mad like hell.

"My mom was just visiting a friend" another said. "It's about time we taught Talin some manners" the crowd raised there swords in the air and chanted Two Swords.

"Now we fight for sure" a voice said behind Reid. He turned around to see the speaker, since it sounded familier to him, it was his sister

"Your not fighting" Reid told her, stubern by the thought of losing her. "alice , I don't want you to fight a man's war".

"Who are you? To speak for me. I 'll fight any creature or man that stands in my way" Alice stood for herself and her fellow females. Reid was lost for words, he knew Alice's past since she was a warrior once and gave it up to raise her nephew.

Reid looked away, a glint was in his right eye. He raised his own weapon and bellowed from the top of his lungs.

"Two Swords unite" as a great cheer surrounded at the top of the tower. People scurried away, gathering supplies and any who didn't have weapons. Many people looked at the surrounding land trying to see Talin's army approaching.

"I see it" a woman yelled as Reid rushed over to her side. He gazed at the size of the army.

"Not a big army" he replied as he shook his head. Nine others shouted for him, he ran toward them all as he called Corp over to him. They never realized that he had sent more than enough.

"Holy" Corp said with amazement at the size of the army. "It's bigger than we thought" but smiled inspite of the thought. "The bigger it is the harder they fall".

Reid didn't like the size of Talin's army but for some reason he felt that were being fooled.

"Corp" Reid called over and the half breed walked only a few steps over to him.

"What is it?" Corp answered.

"Determine the true size of this army, I've a feeling that some of it is an illusion"

"You maybe right" Corp agreed and transformed into the Roc as he dove of the edge. The wind caught him, he flew over the vast army and noticed that Reid was right after all. Only twenty five percent of it was fake, the rest they could handle. Corp flew back and reported his findings.

"He dooped us" Reid said with fury. "How dare he. If that's the game he wants to play, we'll do differently". He turned to the towers side and looked down at the forest.

"Tell Bob to get his troops ready for battle. Cause right now I have to get ready for this battle " Reid stated as he walked away.

Corp flew off once more, down and down he went to the only forest that lay below them. He the others knew the nasty surprise that Talin's army was about to get. Landing infront of rachel a moment later he smiled weakly.

"Prepare the troops, Talin came a littleearly" Corp warned her but Bob had heard his warning. He Frowned at the idea, but he knew that his own troops were getting restless.

"Bout time he showed up, this army is getting bored and restless. Look at them, they're about to fight with each other" Bob declared as Corp turned to see him.

"Don't get cocky, Bob. Talin over estimates us for sure, it will be his undoing in the least" Corp remarked as Bob turned around and smiled.

"You hear that, he thinks Talin will fail on his own" Bob said jokenly. The morph could see the others were in good spirits, his own kind never would have stood up to Talin or any of the other evil creatures nor laugh at them.

"Don't mock him" Corp snapped at him which turned around suddenly. "He's here to kill us, to control our lives and to stop freedom at all costs. Never joke about any of your enemies, cause one day they will destroy you". Bob was stunned by the fury of the morph.

"He's only a man, how much trouble and damage his army can do" Bob retorted smugly.

"Plenty, give him a chance he will show you what

he can do. He's a bully. He teases any that looks different, I know since I went to the same school as him. In every school there is one and by recken I ignored them but it's hard" Corp finished his speech which surprised the whole lot of them. Bob took a few steps toward him.

"I'm so sorry, I had no idea that he teased you that Badly?". Bob said feeling guilty about his own words.

"He did, but I didn't give him a chance to hit me, sometimes it's better to walk away than to confront a bully" Corp pointed out.

Bob understood what Corp was telling him since he alone had confronted a bully from his own school, it turned out that he was a whimp. Now Corp spoke to Rachel as he planed out his attack.

*   *   *

The Tyranny of Talin

As Alice helped her brother dress in his fighting clothes, she knew something was wrong.

"You look terrified, Alice" Reid said calmly with a bit if concern for her.

"I got this feeling that your going to die" Alice remarked as she hugged her brother now.

"I will always be with you in spirit or other wise. I can assure you sis" he tilted his head down towards her cheek, he kissed her as she smiled feeling the pressure of air. A small sound came from it, it sounded like a small fart.

A knock sounded on is door, Reid turned away in time blushing at the thought of kissing his own sister in front of friends.

"Who is it?" she asked.

"Tucker" the immortal said " Is Reid with you maim?" Tucker replied.

"He's right here, pleased come in" Alice remarked and pulled down on his chest plate as Tucker walked into the room. It snapped into place, Reid winched feeling it pinch his skin. Alice flipped it up then set in down once again this time it didn't pinch him. Once that was down Reid picked up his father's old sword.

"Come on Tucker, we got a battle to finish" Reid annouced as his sister looked at him. "May the fury of Esslie continue". She smiled at the thought, she knew what he mint since she was once known as a heroe several years ago.

Standing on a platform in the middle of town, Reid's friends and family with the rest of the villagers looked up at him. He noticed his sister was in full dress as he was. Clearing his voice he scanned the other fighters, and he suddenly realized that he was important. These people were looking up at him, not only as a person but as a leader.

"I may not a King, but I'm the second best. My dad would be better at this" he paused for a few moments as a few people laughed at the comment and of the memory of an old friend. Reid gazed into the eye's of every villager, they were listening to his words since he now commanded them. He felt over joyed by the sight, they still regarden him as a friend but now he was his father's son. The rightful heir and it frightened him to the core. Reid stood there, as his sister strolled up to him no longer afriad.

"This city has been our home for so long and now it's been targeted by Talin. This city will not fall" his voice was amplified through out the city. The enemy looked up at the vast city walls hearing the words spill out of Reid's mouth.

"I will not give up nor be defected by Talin. Our freedom is ours, this city is ours. Now it's your turn Talin, now hear this you shall now fear us for a change. The people of Two Swords are free" he paused once more none laughed he had their attention all right. "FOR OUR FATHERS" he yelled with pride. "Two Swords will stand forever" he finished. Every single person raised their weapons, the warriors below did as well and they all chanted for their success. "Two Swords, Two Swords" they all shouted with glee.

Talin's vast army stared in horror for once, they had never been in a fight with epic portions before.

Seventeen

A Sharp Edge

Swords flung onto other swords, axes to axe or sword to axe. Centaures and every beast that you could ever imagine were battling. Rachel snapped her fingers to see two giant trolls split apart. Blood and guts were everywhere. It looked as if it were a battle to save the entire world but it wasn't at all.

"Rachel behind you" Bob yelled as he struck his sword into a demon.

She turned in time as a blade nearly went through her. She pushed a single drow back with her magic which made the dark elf fly over head only to be stabed in the heart by one of his own kind. Giants killed giants and it was a terrible thing to see but at the same time it looked exciting and trilling. In truth it only meant death , it wasn't a life a normal person wanted. It was for those that loved to kill, at least they usually end up either dead or dieing a horrible death.

Bob jumped up into the air and landed onto one of the evil giants. He stabbed it with his sword, the giant yelled in pain then fell to the ground taking out several orc's. Back on solid ground, he put his sword away as a single drow ran at him. Placing his hands together he smile at the approching drow. His hands spilt apart as did the ground as it raced toward that single drow.

The drow tried to jump out of the way, a bit of the

Ground split toward him. He had no idea, as he then noticed the ground rush past him.

What ever got past the ground attack, the bad guys rushed over to the great city. Floods of gnomes, Troll's, Orges and drow bashed through out the tower city levels.

Humans defended their city, some more seasoned than others but they kept on trying to keep the enemy at bay for the moment.

"Don't kill me" a soldier shouted as a horde of gnomes rushed toward him, taking away his chance of survival.

* * *

Cole knew what he was doing as he looked at the still water that lay within the bowl.

"Kill his followers" he said coldly then felt someone was within his room. He turned to see an old friend of his. "Winlet, it's been a long time" he said coldy.

"It has been to long old friend, I see Talin's army has broken into the city" Winlet answered back enjoying the scene.

"It has, but give it time before Talin's army fails in the attempt. Besides it's nearly midnight now, his power will slip away soon enough" Cole remarked.

* * *

Talin noticed his prey as he stalked past humans as they were defending their great city. Most of it battled the massive force, all kinds of evil beasts lay dead but not their own. He spotted Reid battling an Orc and smiled as the beast fell.

I'm losing, Talin thought. That's insane, I will rule this great and grand city and terrorize those pitiful humans they call fighters.

Reid led him to a single room as he fought Talin's followers, he was making it look like that he never saw him at all. Reid wanted to fight Talin and finsih him for good.

Talin rose his sword since was all ready in his hand, it swung down. Reid blocked the sword with his own and pushed him away. Reid jumped into the air and back flipped over his oppnite and landed. Sword drawn out and clashed it with Talin's only to be blocked himself.

"Give up" Reid said with clenched teeth as he was sweating heavily. Talin circled him as Reid did as well. He noticed a flash of movement which surrounded them. Some one was watching them he noted.

The two kept on fighting what seemed like hours,

sweat poured down their faces. Neither side giving up, Reid thought about his next several moves and noticed how tired Talin was.

"Give it up" Reid said calmly.

"NEVER" Talin snapped "I will rule this city of yours" and smashed Reid's sword away. He back up not knowing what to do but the wall stopped him. Reid saw the blade coming toward him, he moved slightly only to be impaled through his upper arm. Blood gushed out of the wound, as his eye's went wild in agony.

"As long as I'm King, you'll never rule Two Swords" Reid found himself saying. Talin now looked surprised by the words, he had never expected this at all. Grabbing his sword he pulled it out of the arm, Reid winched with pain which fueled his anger.

"Go ahead kill me and see what will happen" he urged the elf. Talin struck out with his sword and impaled him once again, Reid looked down in shock as a sword had indeed pearced his heart.

"Now I am Ruler" Talin said glad that this was over. Reid looked to his right and saw Gemmel walk over to them with his own sword. Reid blacked out from all the pain.

"I've been sane all this time, Talin." Gemmel told him seeing Reid had fallen onto the floor, he needed to act fast before the man died.

"You sane, that's a good one" as Talin watched Reid not willing to turn around to speak to Gemmel. He bonked him over the head with the hilt of the sword which made Talin fall to the floor. He went over to Reid's side and whispered a few words, a double of him appeared beside Reid.

Gemmel knew what he was doing as he picked Reid up in his arms.

"Talin, you've been a noughty boy" Gemmel remarked. "Pity, you'll never see what really happens" as he walked into a shinning light.

In Memory

A crowd of people stood around a single grave murning the loss of there dear friend. Alice cried as did the others, they had never thought that Reid would have fallen from grace. Sorrow filled their hearts as Linda looked at the grave stone which read.

He may was a great King, but he did well.
He was a lover and a fighter, but never
A heroe, he was a good man to the end.
Here lies Reid Crystal.

His wife and son looked down at his grave, both cried their eye's out as Corp stood brave. At least the good guys had won the battle for now.

"We'll miss you, Reid" Corp said as he choked on his words since he was over welmed himself.

* * *

Reid jerked awake as he felt his chest for the first time, He noticed that there wasn't any blood on it.

"I'm not dead then, it was only a dream" Reid said to himself and then noticed a figure in the corner.

"Of caurse not, I have plans for you" the figure said calmly and walked into the small lighted area. Reid looked at the shadow in horror as this mans face was now revealed.

"Winlet" Reid said in surprise.

Sitting down on his new throne, Cole gave a small smile. He was glad to be back within his own chamber at long last, though he had never noticed the red glow under his own throne.

Two of his best servants walked toward him. One had a glass of ale in one hand and the other handed him his dinner. Cole smelled the fish, it was one of his favourt dishes. He grabbed the drink as he leaned back in his throne. Taking a sip of it he smiled at long last, he had forgotten what it was like to smile.

"this is the.... " he started to say.

A terrible explosion rocked the castle, rocks and mortor flew into the air as guards ran toward the throne room in a panic. They noticed that two of their own were dead, a gaping hole was in place where the door used to be. They looked into the throne room and saw to their horror, that their master

had been blown apart along with his own servants.

"Come, quick" one of the guards shouted as they

looked at the room. Everything was torn apart by the explosion.A piece of paper flooted down, one of the guards grabbed it and read the note.

You may have stripped me of my powers brother, but I'm still the victor no matter what you think.

Aride

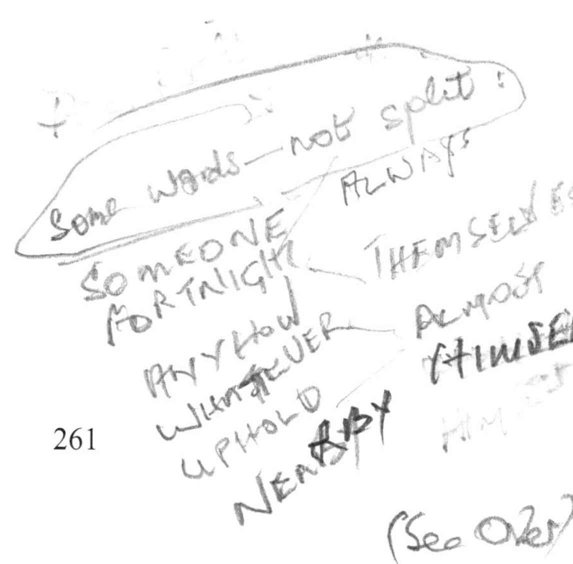

These words should not be split up.

ARROWHEAD
OUTBURST
MAKESHIFT
NAMESAKE
HERSELF
DAYBREAK
OUTCOME
ALREADY
ANYWHERE
MYSELF
upward
downward
whoever
withdraw
WHERABOUTS
SOMEWHAT
Wrongdoers
Outcome
OUTMATCHED
THROUGOUT

Sometime

Summertime
Wintertime
Springtime
Outwards
Inwards
Instead
Bashful
THROUGOUT
CHRISTMAS TIME
SWORDFISH
impOLITE
UNJUST
MISTAKE
NEWSPAPER (OR -N)

POSSESSIVE (Belonging to)

→ his arms were brown

not — her forehead was lined

The ship's deck was crowded

in these simple examples
1. the arms belonged to him
2. The deck belonging to the ship

the alternate to possessive commas is:
her forehead was lined

8804848R0

Made in the USA
Charleston, SC
15 July 2011